RODNEY HALL has twice won the Miles Franklin Award (for *Just Relations* in 1982 and *The Grisly Wife* in 1994) and *The Day We Had Hitler Home* was shortlisted. He was presented with the gold medal of the Australian Literature Society in 1992 and again in 2001. His books are available in half a dozen translations, as well as English editions in the UK and USA.

Other novels by Rodney Hall

Just Relations
Kisses of the Enemy
A Dream more Luminous than Love
    The Second Bridegroom
    The Grisly Wife
    Captivity Captive
The Island in the Mind
    Terra Incognita
    The Lonely Traveller by Night
    Lord Hermaphrodite
The Day We Had Hitler Home
The Last Love Story

Love without Hope

Rodney Hall

Pan Macmillan Australia

First published 2007 in Picador by Pan Macmillan Australia Pty Limited
1 Market Street, Sydney

Copyright © Rodney Hall 2007

The moral right of the author has been asserted.

All rights reserved. No part of this book may be reproduced or
transmitted by any person or entity (including Google, Amazon or
similar organisations) in any form or by any means, electronic
or mechanical, including photocopying, recording, scanning or by
any information storage and retrieval system, without
prior permission in writing from the publisher.

National Library of Australia
Cataloguing-in-Publication data:

Hall, Rodney, 1935– .
Love without hope.

ISBN 978 0 330 42288 8.

I. Title.

A823.3

Set in 11/15.5 pt Stempel Garamond by Midland Typesetters, Australia
Printed in Australia by McPherson's Printing Group

Papers used by Pan Macmillan Australia Pty Ltd are natural, recyclable
products made from wood grown in sustainable forests. The manufacturing
processes conform to the environmental regulations of the country of origin.

The characters and events in this book are fictitious and any resemblance
to real persons, living or dead, is purely coincidental

for Julian Burnside

You are not dying because you are ill. You are dying because you are alive.

Montaigne

Mrs Shoddy has been shouting for an hour. One mightn't think she'd have the will, with all that has happened, yet she shouts. One mightn't think she'd have the strength, brittle and old as she is, yet she shouts – and this shouting provokes a periodic chorus of responses, wailing and mockery from the unseen inmates out there in the dormitory. Even the passageways echo with it. And clatterings and inexplicable hushings happen. But no one comes. All night she has been strapped up to prevent her moving. Her body's desperate need to shift and flex torments her. Isolated and pinned down on a creaky pallet in a concrete room so dim she can scarcely make out the walls, she lies in her own filth and grieves for home, for her farm and her beloved horses. Voice ragged from shouting, she shouts nonetheless. And still no one comes.

Then, without warning, the door swings open for huge shadows to swoop in, each with its attached person, to attack her with wet sponges and towels and unbuckle her buckles and lift what's left of her so they can strip off her threadbare shift, their speech as loud as chaos. Once they've made her decent they fold her into a straitjacket, their elegantly sweeping arms, like those of tennis players intent on victory, winding the tapes to strap her tight. The intruders insist they must erect her. And she finds herself erected. Now they goad her to stagger on stone joints out from the punishment room into the dormitory where she wanted to be – but never wanted to be – where the light itself is enough to fell her at a blow. She winces. Scoured, dressed and trapped between minders, she is hoisted under the armpits and lifted bodily downstairs like an unyielding child.

She is delivered to the office and propped up, face to face with the Master in Lunacy. She thinks, surely his title ought to have been done away with a hundred years ago? This is *nineteen* eighty-three. He doesn't look up. He postpones contact with her blazing eyes. So, for her part, she must own the offence of her shameful condition, helpless with rage and humiliation, too hoarse to speak and too frightened to insist on her rights as a

love without hope

woman of sound mind, a woman wrongly detained.

She remains standing, he remains sitting.

Harsh blades of light slice through the stillness while the Master, experimentally submissive to the demands of a sheet of paper, studies it. Meanwhile, Mrs Shoddy, who would never have been Mrs Shoddy had she not married Mr Shoddy, comforts herself by thinking of Martin: even after all these years Martin might still turn up right when he's most needed. At any moment he could burst in through the door and drag this studious official off his swivel chair, sling him across the desk as he deserves and strangle him with his own tie. Or burst in through the door and stand there, hands in pockets, eyes lazy with contempt. She sees him decide on invective as his weapon rather than violence, lacerating her captors with witty observations concerning the dignity of power and the ethics of justice. She hasn't given up hope, though she doesn't know where he is, or where he has been during the years that have passed since he left her. One thing for sure, he will never tolerate seeing her insulted like this. Never. So even his absence gives her courage. She stands and blazes, though she dare not shout at her persecutors for fear of punishment.

The Master in Lunacy reads in silence and Mrs Shoddy, in silence, watches him read.

She cannot imagine what might occupy such a person's mind, her own being too loaded with worries. Foremost, her anxiety over the horses needing water and needing oats. Needing their coats attended to and their hoofs checked. Needing the comfort of having her around. For their sake, if not her own, she keeps her ears pricked for Martin's footfall. She grows more and more certain that he is on his way. But she hears only the hum of a nearby refrigerator and the more-or-less contented mooing and bellowing of cattle in the slaughter yards down the road. To encourage him to hurry she concentrates on remembering him. Right now, he ought to yank the door open, take her tenderly in his arms, carry her out to his Land Rover, settle her beside him and roar away with her down the convoluted mountain road, across clucking timber bridges over scintillant rivers and deliver her to her duties – the horses fretting at her fence – on the farm where he and she once lived out their bountiful uneasy fervent truce.

At long last the spasms of shivering subside.

'You never had children, Mrs Shoddy?'

She is surprised to find the Master in Lunacy watching her with concerned eyes. She shakes her head. Released into her exhaustion, this is all she can manage. If they had let her sleep she might not feel so whacked. But now it's a minuscule thing that steals her attention, a mere glimmer of light, pale blue, reflected in the brass nameplate on the Master's desk. The tremendous importance of this blueness is that she knows its source: the ogre close behind her. She knows that he looms over her. Indeed, she smells the starch of his regulation blue cotton jacket and her flesh cringes from the heat he gives out. He stands too close. He is colossally present. His breath tumbles down about her ears in cloudy black rocks even as she finds her voice, at last.

'What have you,' she croaks, 'done to me?'

And only now does she read the Master in Lunacy's name etched into the brass: *Mr Bevis Radcliffe*. And watches him take up a pen.

'According to your file,' he says, poised ready to write but not writing, 'you have nobody. Is that correct?'

Behind her the stalker lets his hand touch her shoulder briefly, as if to nudge her into a satisfactory reply. But she needs to speak out about the plight of her horses and the horror of her nightmares.

O Martin, come now!

Light from the tall windows slants in through deep casements to seek her out. The old flock wallpaper painted over with a coat of ugly cream paint, through which the flowering sprigs still show as phantom lumps and veins, is a relic of those leisured times when this was a homestead on the outskirts of town. The room has no breath in it: people, but no breath.

I am not mad, she repeats in her mind.

A telephone shrill-shrills. The Master in Lunacy drops his pen. He closes his eyes with exasperation and his face appears younger that way. His hand knows exactly where the phone is and takes it up like something which *she* might have touched already, something soiled.

'I'm busy.'

Mrs Shoddy comes to her senses. Behind her the cotton jacket rearranges itself around a wearer whose name is embroidered on the pocket. She remembers it without turning to look. She remembers the stitching and the chest panels hammered on, the short sleeves extruding lumps of meat, the roundness and bentness of arms. *Vernon*.

'Ring me later.'

The Master flips the receiver back on its cradle and again reveals his concerned but disillusioned eyes. Older at a stroke, he occupies himself extracting a sheaf of papers from her file. Perhaps he slept badly, much like herself. Sympathy stirs within her as he selects a sample page, spinning it (as if on a turntable) to display the message so she can see for herself. She leans to peer at handwriting no more readable than ruffled shadows among the waves at sea and no more stable either. Salt stings her eyes. But she cannot wipe them. The straitjacket binds her in.

'Um,' she says, though she knows the issue is desperate.

'You asked to see your admission papers, Lorna. Goodness knows why. But I'm a reasonable man. So here you are. It is my duty to inform you that this committal can be contested, upon application by a close relative, and referred to our own psychiatric review process. Then, of course, there is the final court of appeal, the Administrative Decisions Tribunal.'

The elements gather round Mrs Shoddy: a glass-fronted bookcase with a typewriter on top, a varnished desk, a rotating rack of rubber stamps, two steel filing

love without hope

cabinets and the shut door beside them, slashed glimpses of a garden and a yard beyond, one direct needle of light piercing the blinds. This is her chance to give voice to her pain and betrayal – it's an outrage that you brought me here – but she only recognises her opportunity at the very moment it begins to escape her. Before the chance is altogether lost she must seize the Master's attention and expose the system he is part of. After all, these troubles began with an insult as simple as women arriving with an unasked-for lunch. She must speak. Her horses need her.

'Things got too expensive,' she mumbles. That's not right. That doesn't matter. True though it is. And maybe my troubles really did begin because I boggled at the price-stickers in the corner store. Unbelievable prices for simple things like corned beef, for goodness' sake, and corn. Her blood ebbs wearily.

'Those women,' she weeps, 'started . . . coming round.'

'You mean the volunteers bringing you meals? Or the nurses?'

'Snooping in at my windows.'

He withdraws the document out of range of her snivelling.

'You need to be in care. That's the long and short of it.'

'My husband . . .'

'Ah, yes, the husband, Mrs Shoddy.'

The Master restores his evidence to the safety of the file where it belongs and then proceeds to inspect his own manicured hands, as displayed on an acreage of desktop. He selects what needs to be said.

'You tell us there is a husband. A *Mr* Shoddy, perhaps. But we can do no more than consult the births, deaths and marriage records. And the records show nothing to support such a claim.'

Well, of course not, Martin would never set foot in a church, let alone the banality of a registry office. She has his ring. The ring should be enough. But, when she finds she can't move her arms or show her hands, she knows she is in a dream. She used to joke about the masculine aspect of her character, well, she must have lost it. Or somehow the fact that she's tied up incapacitates her mind as well as her body. Not for a moment can she forget the straitjacket. Her weeping gets worse. And, when she tries to speak, she bubbles.

'We have little alternative, therefore, but to conclude,' the Master in Lunacy concludes, 'that there is no one to whom we may refer the issue of your care. That is to say, your *ongoing* care.'

Hopeless though it is, she struggles to extricate her hands from the nightmarish crampy garment that binds her arms across her stomach like a mummy. She totters, losing her balance. But the steel-plated Vernon-blue tunic bulks up against her, while the ogre's Vernon-hands seize her shoulders, unable to resist giving her a bit of a warning shake as he sets her back upright for further consideration by her benefactor. A breeze from the sun-struck garden traces lavender-perfumed tracks down her cheeks, confirming the tired and wrinkled state of her face. She, who was once that hearty little horsewoman, recognises herself as reduced to a tiny stick-person with twig hands and bark for skin, perhaps scarcely even recognisable. Her animals, however, would still know her. A horse looks into your soul, its eye magnifying the proud lustrous purpose of journeys. A horse is not fooled. Her mares would remember how she attended them when their foals were delivered, helping with gentle massage, her fingers working the slimy fluid to ease their stress, feeling for the swell of energy in those bulging slow pulsations and the climactic expulsion of a veiled spooky head-heavy infant unfolding soft-boned legs to stagger up and fight free of the glutinous membrane and to cough its first breath of terror.

'No one,' the Master in Lunacy repeats, 'so I'm afraid there is little to be gained from prolonging this interview.'

And, with that, he allows a faint semblance of regret to corrupt his smile. Behind his back, garden flowers crowd to the window. She remembers once, when she was a child, holding an injured pigeon and feeling its heart beat and how easily she prevented its wings from opening, though she felt them shift in her grasp. The memory fills her with shame. How the dumb foolish creature gaped and blinked in distress. Blink. And the thought of that bird-eyelid (so frail a utility, as perfectly formed as her own) being its only means of countering the crisis shocks her.

'My house!' she screams, syllables quite other than she expected to come upon.

The ogre has her by the shoulders, though what can he do? Can he kill her?

'My horses!' she screams.

And this is more like it. So even the Master in Lunacy, patting his bald head, offers her a watery nod of approval.

'Horses,' he says, 'figure somewhat prominently in your file.'

Vernon still grips her shoulders. And she has the sense that Vernon's fingers know what she is about to do before she herself knows, being informed by long practice at quelling the struggles of so many of the baffled.

'Who are you,' she murmurs, daring, 'to take away ... everything?' And she connects it with those well-intentioned stickybeaks who bore down on her with steamy dishes under tin covers. 'Or to *give*, for that matter?'

The man who holds her fate in his paperwork jots a note to himself. Then looks up, expecting more. His glossy head a dome.

'By *coming here*, you mean,' the Master in Lunacy enquires eventually, having left a discreet silence to demonstrate that without his help her questions inevitably die in the space between them, 'to this psychiatric hospital?'

'I was thinking of my father,' she answers calmly. 'And his father.'

love without hope

'Ah.'

The tears have dried on her cheeks and tiny crustings now lace the slack flesh to hold it in that look of sadness. She need not attend to it. The pride of decency can fill her now. Words come strongly.

'Who has the right to take a person's home?'

The lavender air fills her, as she fills the straitjacket – so if you were to slice through her you would slice wafers of mauve bee-blessed comfort. As for the Master, he looks her over closely, at this juncture, much the way a handyman might examine an article of furniture, appraising how it is put together. Such is his skill with mitre-box and chisel, his look informs her, he might make any number of such objects at whim. He places a hand on his naked head, like the hanging judge putting on his cap to pronounce judgement.

'*This* is now your home. And I believe I can assure you that no one will take it away from you.'

When Rita Gibbons runs into Gail Savage wheeling her supermarket trolley up to the meat fridge (this new shop brings credit to a town of no more than eight hundred) she smiles with just that touch of genteel reserve she prides herself on. Eyeing Gail's choice of sausages, she knows her duty.

'Is that for you or for *them*?'

'For Russell.'

Russell, the awful husband.

'That brand you got there,' she observes with the impartiality of the ruling class, 'is no better than junk food. I saw on the TV. But, then, a modern diet might not suit you. Where me and Mr Gibbons is concerned we've given up the fats and sugars. Not to mention salt.' Her gaze having fetched up against a mirror (one of those backing mirrors put in to double the stock of goods on display) she spares a glance for her own stupendous bosom sheathed in non-iron florals, orange and green. 'All boils down to education is what I say.'

Gail pops the sausages back in the fridge. Anything for a quiet life. Easier to avoid having to justify her choices . . . let alone her motives. Instead, she considers some loin chops.

'Mind you,' Rita concedes, 'the TV itself is pretty much junk, in a manner of speakin'.'

'Isn't that the truth! Except for the soaps. I follow the soaps.'

'Not me. I've seen too much of real life.'

The lamb will surely do?

'Such prices they put on meat in this place!' Rita punctuates her disapproval with a snap of false teeth.

Gail dithers a moment before conceding the point and exchanging the chops for some cheaper pork flap.

'Just as well it's not for *their* dinner,' Rita advises while setting her trolley in motion, somewhat satisfied when Gail follows. 'Mrs Brady, for one, might be a Jew.' Besides the advantage of impressive bulk, Rita is old enough to be Gail's mother. 'Though *that* – what you've got – 's for Russell, you say. Well, I don't suppose Russell's a Jew!'

She sheds a few hiccups of laughter.

Despite being next-door neighbours the two women have little in common. And if it weren't for meals-on-wheels they would probably seldom bother with the niceties. Really, the difference goes back to Rita's great-grandparents who pioneered the district during the days of first settlement, because this sets her apart and supplies the source of her authority. No matter what comes her way, she's the equal.

Gail, poor thing, seems quite without family at all. And quite without judgement, too. She may have been pretty at some stage, but she can no longer rely on that. Faded sandy eyelashes and a wandering mouth give her away as the nobody she is, a nobody of forty or more, with tender little breasts and freckled arms. The breasts being the last survival of her youth, unless you count neat ankles and firm calves. The mere thought of those calves sets Rita's grey hair standing on end around her headache, besides agitating her hands till the little old diamond on her finger comes good with a few faint twinkles. Well, Rita tells herself, *noblesse oblige*. In a volunteer organisation one cannot choose one's associates. And credit where credit's due, Gail is a worker. For that reason alone a certain shared contentment can be allowed – no harm done.

'All this other stuff you got,' she supposes, giving Gail's trolley a little nudge with her own, 'is for today's offerin's for the oldies?'

'Yes, it is.'

love without hope

'Well, don't forget the receipt for what you spend.'

The civilities having been observed, Rita now licenses her hand to dive right in, sorting through her companion's shopping, item by item, raising her eyebrows and sucking in her cheeks as she makes swift calculations of the total cost to the CWA. This is their twice-weekly routine. Once the purchases are made Gail will spend the entire morning cooking, ready for the two of them to set out in the Ford, bearing the gift of lunch to their clients: Gerry Boyd, retired axeman, never married, who looks forward to his ninetieth birthday alone with whatever choice of cake they might bring, Grannie Osborne at the dairy farm (though she no longer has any cows in her paddocks), Miss Valerie Hughes, a former school mistress and hockey aficionado, Mrs Colonel Brady, surrounded by photographs of her husband in uniform and overwhelmed by his shelf of books on the decisive battles of the world, her neighbour Mrs Jessie Forrester, the dear thing, loved by all, plus a new one, that strange woman out beyond the fringe of town, Mrs Shoddy. Everyone knows her as the horse lady, but no one talks to her. Besides, she's a peril on the road because she insists on driving herself into town at twenty kilometres an hour, perched on the seat of her Land Rover, though so small she's only able to peer out through the spokes of the steering wheel, liable to appear round any corner, travelling with scarcely a puff of dust, a vacant stare of foreboding on her face. Except that, according to rumour, she has not been sighted since Friday. Frankly, the ladies don't know whether she is expecting their service or not.

Anyhow, the remaining five are the acknowledged regulars. And that's quite enough to cook for, Mrs Shoddy or no Mrs Shoddy. And quite enough to buy for, though the Country Women's Association meets the cost of ingredients and the gas to cook on. Without the CWA none of this would happen at all. And, since being elected President and volunteering to help out on the meals committee, Rita – as champion of frugality and spokeswoman for the established families of the district – has found herself more-or-less obliged to supervise the whole operation, which she does from the vantage point of a clipboard with a schedule and her Discharge Book, where each delivery of comfort is recorded and properly signed off.

'So, if it's not the pork flap, what are they to be fed today, Gail?'

'Shepherd's pie and mash.'

'With Brussels sprouts?'

'With *these* sprouts, don't you think?'

Their trolleys, on wayward wheels, clash again, giving Rita's tub of fat-free yogurt a jolt. But Gail isn't the sort to notice. She is too absorbed in thought, having observed how pale Rita looks, especially for such an indestructibly maternal person with those vast pendulous breasts. Though she can't really warm to Rita Gibbons's temperament, she worries.

'Are you sleeping all right?' Gail says timidly.

'What do you think?' says Rita rudely, being such a public migraine sufferer that her bedside light has often been known to stay on well past midnight.

'I hoped,' says Gail, 'for your sake.' Thinking that it mightn't be too long before Rita's name turns up among the clients. Though heaven help any nurse given the job of turning her over in bed for a wash and clean-up! Gail no sooner lets this thought take shape than she's afraid it might be read in her eyes.

'So, will you meet me at the kitchen?' she suggests, patting her unruly ginger curls in place and taking the trouble to produce the CWA hall key (there being this uneasiness between them) as proof of her good intentions.

'At half past,' Rita Gibbons confirms as she turns her back and goes rocking away, from one stiff hip to the other, taking her place in the check-out queue behind the publican, who greets her sympathetically so he can complain about his own bad leg. During a bit of a hold-up while the price of some unmarked item is disputed he seizes the chance to sketch in the whole catalogue of his disabilities.

'Truly?' says Rita. 'Truly?'

'My word,' he assures her. 'And the pain's a killer.'

'You poor thing,' says Rita who, despite feeling a bit faint herself, registers that his grievances are the same as last time she heard.

'I'm prone to the odd turn myself,' she confides.

But it's not what he wants to hear. He wants to be told

about himself so he can get a grip on things. He gets busy unloading his basket and he doesn't invite her to elaborate, a discourtesy she takes note of and resents.

'This leg . . .' he whines.

'Tell Dr Parker, not me,' she cuts him short sharply.

'But you know what, Rita?' He grows conspiratorial. 'I've switched over to the new chap.'

'The young doctor?' she says enviously, because this is an idea she herself never entertained. Though, who knows? And why not? Maybe some miracle cure for migraine has been discovered while Archie Parker, too stuck on his traditional remedies, not to mention his gin, remains in ignorance.

'There's things going on,' the publican adds mysteriously, as if everyone (himself included) is entitled to keep what they are hiding hidden, 'that our new doctor . . . knows about.' He puts a finger up to his lips and she recollects that these same lips kissed hers about fifty years ago. Then he scoops his change off the counter and leans away, canting out through the glass door into the sunlit street.

Rita calls, 'Bye-bye, Gail,' when her own turn comes.

And Gail, down near the biscuits, looks up and waves. But still she can't decide on Russell's dinner and she relinquishes the pork in favour of those sausages. Suddenly it strikes her that she is afraid of him, not just because he hits her from time to time, but afraid that this is not the worst he can do. Her trolley grinds from aisle to aisle with her in tow. She thinks – and thinks – quite lost to the moment. Wheeling round an island of detergents, all on special, and along a gallery of soft drinks where a group of locals have gathered to gossip in undertones, she collides with the district nurse, the very person she has just imagined in the act of struggling to turn a mountainous and bedridden Rita. The jangling trolleys lock at right angles.

'Hullo,' Olga exclaims in surprise, disengaging her wheels as if somehow caught out.

Gail, taken aback for a moment, says nothing. Then she recollects herself. 'What news of Mrs Shoddy?' she thinks to enquire. 'Is she expecting her meal today?'

'Why ask me,' Olga retorts, adding with disgust, almost to herself, 'in such a public place?'

'I suppose I thought you'd be the one to know.'

'Well, I'm not. It's not just a health issue. It's out of my hands.'

Delivering herself of this finality, Olga stalks off without another word, her blonde ponytail swishing indignantly.

Vernon carries Mrs Shoddy bodily and shuts her away again in that dark little room. He straps her flat on the pallet. She, who always slept on her face. And, such is his expertise, he completes the task without bruising her.

'We are here to help,' he tells her while he works, 'but we don't have to put up with your rantings, Lorna. Just be satisfied: you asked once, now don't ask to see the boss a second time.'

To this she says nothing. She understands the rebellion in her silence. He can only contest accusations that

love without hope

she puts into words. Her silence remains her own. She shuts him out.

'Have it your way,' Vernon snaps.

And goes. He crashes the reinforced door closed, leaving her sealed in darkness.

'I shall not panic,' she mutters to herself, 'I shall sleep.'

Sleep, like silence, is her defence. And sleep will help speed Martin's return. But the nightmare haunting Mrs Shoddy is that she may never sleep again. Already her body cries out for release, for the freedom to move. What ever did I do to deserve losing the farm? That's another question she should have asked the Master in Lunacy. How could she have remained so tongue-tied, so shut off from her commonsense needs as to neglect getting an answer? So, she must sleep, if only to play for time. Horses, of course, manage standing up. That's their way. She thinks of herself on rigidly locked legs and what it might be like to have the gift. Then there are those species of bird that sleep on the wing, the colossal condor for example, gliding over an eternal sea of snow-capped mountains, sustained only by wind and a peculiar ability to let the mind go with all its fears and calculations of peril. Not able to stand, she tries flying.

'Was it something I said?'

The room is so sealed that only the slenderest filaments of light make their way through the cracks.

'Don't ask questions,' she rebukes herself. 'Just survive.'

And, flying, she dreams of somebody coming to check on her, somebody rostered on the afternoon shift, who apologises for the mistake and assures her the authorities thought she was someone else, some altogether mad person needing restraint. And she dreams of being led out to a table where fruit is set ready in a bowl beside a tumbler of cool water.

'That's rubbish!' Mrs Shoddy shouts.

She needs to deal with reality. Yes, but the present reality must not be her future. She cannot continue like this. In this agony. Not even for another day.

'I wasted all those years,' she moans. 'Every hour squandered.'

Yes, as she thinks it through, she had thousands of opportunities to escape the district since Martin went, to have her darlings trucked out somewhere else, somewhere not brooded over, or spied on, somewhere less haunted by spirits, too. Her needs were simple.

'Just a hut,' she concedes.

Surely she could have thought of that when she had free use of her legs – a rudimentary hut that the stickybeaks would not find even if they tried – when she had a key for her vehicle and petrol in the tank. Thousands of days wasted arguing the toss with petty tyrants behind cash registers and tyrants bringing plates of food. Years and years. All gone. While she naively frittered the precious time on gazing at sunrises and sunsets, on telling the horses her love when they knew, they already knew and had known since the day they were born. She

love without hope

sees them in her mind, foal-lipped, seeking the source of the mare's milk even while their trusting eyes watch her hover near and . . .

The electric light snaps on, drowning her in a surveillance of dazzling atoms. She winces behind bird-lids. Someone comes in the door. Then before she can tolerate opening her eyes again, the light snaps off. She hears a squeak of departing rubber shoes.

'Who?' she trembles.

She hears the lock chuckle. No one. No one is here but herself. She struggles against the straps. But the only freedom to move is in the memory. So much that seemed ordinary at the time is now like a glittering mirage. The places and the people. And to think how her mother used to worry on her behalf, altogether for the wrong reasons: *love* wasn't what she'd missed out on, as it transpired. What she missed was finding an answer to whether or not Martin had done something in his life to make him so different from other men. Done something, that is to say, terrible. She remembers his warm silky skin, his carelessly shaved cheek and muscular throat. As for that faint reek of the demonic, maybe it was no more than his lack of manners and nothing to worry about. He was a sinner, beyond question, an exuberant sinner and eager for trouble. Surely, the lost years won't have changed him? Nothing about Martin being superfluous. The superfluous, only, ages. She can believe him immune, still with youthful black brows and black eyes in contrast to that curious ivory complexion. Even after exposure to the fiercest summer sun he only ever showed a slight flush of pink, while she herself, plump and rosy and brown, sat snug in the saddle and laughed down at him as he held the bridle to detain her, encountering so much love in his eyes she half expected him to kiss her boot before she could dig her heels in to set the cushioned pastures skittering and spinning behind her, the rhythm of her horse's hoofs drawing music from the dusty road all the way down to the sea. Though, equally, he was quite capable of giving the horse a vicious slap on the rump to frighten it just so he could poke fun at her discomfiture. Or, perhaps, he might extract a worn-cornered book from his hip pocket, open it and read out, as his farewell, a poem she already knew by heart:

When bright Orion has declined
His aim obliquely from the Pole,
And darkness taken full control
Of earth and sleeping humankind,

Stampeding from the wastes behind,
The skewbald nightmare and her foal
Plunge their great hoofs and caracole
Against the fences of the mind.

Mrs Shoddy struggles against the straps, exhausted. She drifts on the thermals. Drops of rain may amount to a drenching, she thinks like an incantation, or a mere patter on canvas, as reassuring as the sociability of cows at night. Martin had, perhaps, killed someone. Or invented the new secret language of crime. Or another sort of music. He came into her life from nowhere. And went out of it nowhere. Yet the years between his coming and his going were the years in which she knew herself and knew she was desired.

Not that he told her he loved her. They spoke their love every time they discussed harnesses and lunging-reins, or the pastures even. And love illuminated both their lives. Why else would she miss him so? Why else would her whole substance have come unravelled at the first touch of something as ordinary as flames? She had been through enough bushfires before, for goodness' sake. What else but the loss of him could paralyse her, leave her fixed and helpless at her open front door, when she glimpsed the forested horizon as a black silhouette against the conflagration lighting up the whole night? It was a big one. That's all. So, what prevented her driving her vehicle to any of the neighbourhood farms to seek news of the wind, the direction of the front, to ask if they'd telephone the transport people to bring some horsefloats – even a livestock truck? Beyond doubt, it was the happiness she had once known. That was what rendered her helpless through the small hours before dawn.

This bushfire leapt her way, raging up from the south, to put an end to the life she knew. It stormed the hill, exploding to puffs of ignited scrub, the bronzed glare of morning sun plastering the whole scene with malevolent magic, till a vast incandescent tumbleweed, a living ball of flame and popping gases, rolled on the thermal of its own creation, a heat gale sweeping ahead so that dead and living leaves, grass tufts and stumps spontaneously flared up, transmuted to the element of wind – as if already no more substantial than the assembled ash of what they were about to become – not even waiting for the touch of the flames that followed. And she found her horses, teeth bared, backing away to huddle against the northern fence, where they collided as cushions of muscle, flanks shuddering and hoofs knocking sharply as they jostled to be let out. There was no gate on that northern boundary. So she had run and stumbled, her old shirt fluttering and hampering her. She had shrieked at them to follow, cajoling, entreating, cursing, to persuade them back into the open so she could just slip a chain and let them free.

Just this once they shied away and reared up against her begging voice, her fire-flushed face and hammered eyes, her harsh imperious cries sounding like a desperate eagle, she'd flung the west gate open, only to be bowled over by tidal smoke, from which she unburied herself to stagger again to the rescue. *Now* could they see there was a way out? No, they could not. If only they might agree to back away from the fence they should be able to take a run at it and leap over. But when she reached for them again they shrank from her hand, corralled and crushed by a wall of heat. Panicking, they refused to be guided or driven a single step the other way. She saw, in their eyes, that they believed they were running already, even

love without hope

while clustered in a trapped pack against the wire. She had failed them.

She sank against a fence post. A sweep of flame arrived. They were on fire and screaming with pain. On her knees she watched, felled by a surge of anger against their stubborn impotent stupidity, those intelligent animals, when there in the grass she found an old pair of pliers, pliers abandoned by her father or by Martin. Whichever. Pliers from God. Just what she needed. Immediately she struggled to cut the thick fence wire. She'd got the grip. Thrashing her solid shoulders about, the weight of her capable body thrust to and fro as the blunt cutting blades bit. And finally, with the *thwok* of a whip, the top strand gave.

Her horses, with fiery manes and coats smoking, some with raw patches suppurating already, leapt to freedom, cantering away among the tall trees, heedless of fallen logs and rabbit holes, down to the creek and the sea. Then it was just herself left behind in the embrace of flame, with the flash of ice-fire, as she turned her scaled eyes blindly for escape, stumbled across to the horse trough, took a deep breath and plunged in, one foot skidding on the slimy rim, cracking her shin unnoticed, and wallowing there while the oxygenless miasma rushed over and a canopy of cinders a mile thick drew down the sky with its catastrophe of tumbling insects swept in a vortex beyond the extremity of breath, no sooner there than gone, so that when she broke through the surface skin of water, up and out from that placenta of horse-saliva and burnt leaf-oil to cough herself back to life, the inferno had passed. A bell of silence clapped itself down over the blackened trees and turf, her world curling at the edges and noiselessly crepitating, little spits of silence dodging among the ashes. At last the roar of receding fire reached her. And she heard the hundred-voiced cattle from her neighbour's farm bellow hoarse blares of alarm, maddened beasts.

Though scorched, the smoke-reeking house had been spared, her orderly house of polished furniture and folded linen. Shaken, she took to her bed. And much later heard rifle shots down in the valley. When eventually she rose she never knew who had led her three surviving horses back or mended her fence (she didn't ask, because she couldn't bear hearing what state the other horses were in and why they'd had to be put down, nor even the intrusion of affability that must follow: the *gratitude* for her loss). Now and again she crept to the kitchen, leaving behind the first unwashed dishes, the first litter of scraps, the beginnings of an abandonment she must tolerate to make room for her new fragility.

Once, but once only, she included a visit to the doctor on her wavering journey to town, Dr Parker, old Archibald Parker, because, as she told him, there was no reason why she should be feeling so tiny, peaked as she'd grown, and her clothes billowing around her, hairs scattering from her head and unable to feel anything with her fingertips. In his kindly way – though his mind remained

love without hope

focused on the prospect of a stiff gin soon to be earned – he offered routine questions for her attention and scratched the nape of his neck at so many whispered negatives, until, at last, after the best part of an hour and positively gaping with desperation, he brought his deductive acumen up against the repeated notion of the bushfire.

'Shock,' he'd said sagely. 'The shock triggered this. You are suffering from profound clinical depression.'

With which her tears had agreed, tears so astonishing to him, because, as everyone knew, there was no more competent farm woman within forty kilometres. To free himself for plunging into his medical manual he'd shaken off all siren hopes of a drink. Of course, he cared. Of course, he felt gratified that she trusted him and that, unlike so many others, she had not gone over to the new doctor – a rival who had hung out his shingle despite warnings that the population was too small to support more than one practice. Jack Boswell's family were old patients and Lorna still remained loyal to him even as Mrs Shoddy. He'd passed her his handkerchief... and she had known then that he would help. Indeed, he'd even telephoned a colleague in Melbourne, saying little but listening deeply.

'This is what's commonly known as Diogenes syndrome. It is treatable,' he'd assured her when the call finished. 'Although there are potential side-effects, we do have a good drug, a tricyclic antidepressant. It's new. Despite the drawbacks this is what I'm recommending.'

He wrote a prescription, which he handed over to her. 'The numbness in your fingertips, however, may never repair itself.' At which she'd nodded to show that he shouldn't interrupt the dreadful logic of her life-sentence with any confusing softeners. 'Meanwhile, we should build you up with nourishing food. Steak, butter, spinach, that sort of thing.'

He'd added one more detail: 'This probably began years ago when Martin left. And all it needed was a trigger. Does he know?'

But by then she was already in full flight. She had fled. She had gone before her body could get up on wonky pins to follow. She had pitched down the front steps well before her hand could pull the surgery door closed behind her or let go so the doorknob might glow like a dim brass moon against the dark timber panelling. Once outside, she confirmed the deadness of her skin, feeling no hint of the wind that disturbed Dr Parker's garden. What did it mean for nerve-ends to die? Down in the street she sensed the truth that her flesh did indeed no longer connect her to the world by receptively touching: her skin had grown insensitive like an insect's carapace. She could explain herself as dwindling backward through time into childsized shoes, tightening a length of cord round the bunched waist of her jodhpurs, perching on the seat of her Land Rover and proceeding homeward ever more tentatively behind the flat shatterable glass of the windscreen, pushing before her the vast weight of what her numb hands could no longer feel.

love without hope

Only afterwards did she remember she had neglected to pay.

And, later that afternoon, when she dared present herself to her horses, dear creatures – who must surely be repelled by the change in her – she found her favourites sucking at the slime in the trough where she had lain with bottled breath. She was so proud of breeding them, Australian Walers, once called the best saddle horse in the world. And so they were, with their well-sprung ribs and powerful quarters, their agility and stamina. Cranking her courage to the limit now, she had dared rest her reaching wooden fingers on their necks, terrified that they would not know her, only to find they nuzzled against her with their wide nostrils, knocking her off-balance in the recognition of love's unchangeability and the soul's cry for companionship. They had forgotten the fire already.

Lorna Shoddy lies strapped on the pallet, forced to face the ceiling, unable to move, disoriented by darkness, numb and tearless, the power to feel having lodged itself in her bones – the flesh shrivelled and juiceless – and still she cries out for the fellowship of those horse friends, the weight of their great placid equine heads seeking a moment's rest on her shoulders.

Olga Ostrov parks her car at the gate to Mrs Shoddy's farm – even a little outside it – because she is superstitious. No doubt she inherited this superstition, along with her straight nose, from her Ostrovsky forebears. True, on one level, she admits that she lodged her report with the doctor, also that she was aware of some documentation being completed, yes, and she knew an ambulance had been called a couple of days ago because she herself saw it driving through town. Yet, on another level, she fiercely denies being privy to any *actual* information on the matter. Keeping her options open, she does not put a name to her role in the affair (apart from calling it, perhaps, *duty of care*), let alone putting a name to what this may have set in motion. She has come, simply, so she can rest easy, sure the right thing is being done. And she climbs the rough gravel drive with a clear conscience.

Yet the curious lull of Mrs Shoddy's neglected orchard seems somehow threatening. The old girl's Land Rover stands to one side, stopped at an awkward angle, as if abandoned by chance. Olga falters. The house itself waits alert, windows attentive, a hushed receptacle of listening. Normal noises, unnaturally augmented by the hush, strike her as grotesque: the flitter of squabbling magpies noisily rustling dead hydrangea heads. An aeon later the remote cackle of unseen kookaburras grates on the ear. Shadows map the land with permanent blotches. The lull catches her off guard. The stillness is alive.

Word has got out – as word inevitably does in country towns – that the Council may foreclose in the matter of Mrs Shoddy's unpaid rates (rates going back many years, by all accounts), also that the court orders served on her were repeatedly ignored. In every aspect a sorry story. Well, events do tend to take their course, as Olga herself puts it. The system, you might say, makes up its own mind. That's what public records are for. Olga braces herself. Her training backs her up because, apart from competence, she has the experience, as all would acknowledge, of caring for a whole parcel of geriatrics.

And these old people show gratitude, so the story goes. She is loved.

Last week when she came her visit was official, in response to a citizen request. Now, by contrast, peace of mind seems to elude her. With nothing to investigate, even though she may claim that it's a routine call, what has she become? Olga draws a deep breath. Nonsense! Decisively, she approaches the front door. Some childhood taboo kicks in. Some Russian credulousness. She dares not try it. A surge of trepidation (awe almost) crowds her mind with reservations. She chooses the side path instead and walks between lines of stones which at one time bordered flowerbeds. She sees her white shoes as not belonging here. Suddenly, so it seems, she scarcely likes to let them touch the gravel for the noise they make, even arching her feet. She glances up. At that moment, a wide vista of paddocks glides into view, beautiful beyond all anticipation. A hawk is a golden stud in the sky. The watertank freezes with sunlight.

The farm lies vulnerable to her comprehensive view, pastures sweeping downhill, neatly stitched by fences, studded with occasional trees, a hundred acres of quiet, nestled in surrounding bushland under the glorious painted morning. And, away on the horizon, a flat ocean shimmers. That mad woman's modest farmhouse overlooks this magnificent prospect.

Olga is transfixed.

To think of the crazy old chook waking each morning to this! Temptation already a yeast in her brain, she

love without hope

knows she must not trespass into such hopes. She must make do with impunity, plus her own modest satisfactions. Somewhere in her head she collides with her secret self. Yet her covetousness gazes about her even as she takes up the expedition again . . . and an expedition it has become. Beyond reach of safety, she has already advanced too far. A tiny breeze starts up somewhere down near the creek, darting across the gates to make its coiling interrogative way around the back of her neck. Startled, she becomes conscious of watchers. Snoopers. She knows, she suspects. Convinced that witnesses with cameras are snapping her picture. Guardians with tape-recorders taking note of her intrusion. Yes, down there. Where?

She can see nothing but three horses at the fence silently questioning her with great still eyes. Her shock etches them, like outlines cut in bevelled glass. They do not move. An isolated muscle shudders down one golden-brown haunch. That's all, and a black tail whisks intruding flies away at a single sweep. Utterly absorbed in watching her, the horses know she has no right. They recognise. They deduce. And, by their unconcern, they also register her lack of courage. This is the mortifying shaft pinning her to the spot: to them she does not matter. Even though she absorbs their attention and piques their curiosity, she is a person of no account.

'Shoo!' she cries, her voice strangled by apprehension that someone, apart from the horses, might somehow hear.

Yet not one among those great bronze beasts so much as flinches. And she doesn't care to expose her impotence a second time. She simply turns her back, as the best she can do. She finds herself facing the kitchen door... which stands open. Fear clutches at her. Crackling hairs escape her ponytail. Is some person in there? Do the rumours of a husband have some substance? Might there be a Mr Shoddy, axe in hand, about to stride out to his labours, arrested by the sight of her and lurking in the shadows, waiting to see what her intentions are? Or is he out in the fields already? Or in the shed? Olga glances about nervously. Or is he among the trellises of the neglected orchard? She discovers that her hand is covering her mouth. She suppresses palpitations and calms her troubled heart. Nonsense. He has been gone so long that none of the neighbours can even describe him. The next-door farmer, the one who rescued Mrs Shoddy's horses after the fire, told her his opinion that the husband was nothing but a rumour his own mother had made up just after the war.

Olga steps to the threshold where a blade of darkness slices off her enquiring face. With one hand she reaches in, up to the elbow in the chill of emptiness, to knock. Bone on wood. The announcement of her arrival evokes nothing. She hears the flies, swarms of flies, busy in there. Has someone died?

'Coo-ee,' she croaks.

But she knows Mrs Shoddy cannot be inside. Mrs Shoddy is the one person who categorically cannot rush

love without hope

out to surprise her. Mrs Shoddy has been taken away. The waiting music, tapping out each spaced note, is the drip of water into a sink... *plick... plick*. Her vision glides ahead like a looming horror-film camera. Soon sharp violins will screech and kettledrums shock her with a tumultuous tattoo of heartbeats. Soon she will come upon the one thing she has not imagined: a mutilated body, a leering monster, a skeleton. Yet Olga's vice grips her still. She is addicted. She steps in.

'Mrs Shoddy,' she whisper-calls, trying out her nerve.

The flies immediately attend to her face and hands, they cluster on her neck and investigate her lips and nose. She fights them off in distress. Even so, forcing herself to stand her ground. She has come this far. She can watch her own outline as a dark ghost in the glass-fronted cabinet. Distortions of the ghost, as she moves, swell from her head and grow mounds and lumps on her shoulders, besides eating hollows from her arms. In the stillness of warped shapes and the brooding hostility something lurks undisclosed.

The truth hits her then: *she* is thinking all this. I am here in Mrs Shoddy's dream.

'I will not have it,' Olga says. Proof of reality being the sound made by her advancing shoes. Yes, and she is getting the idea now that she can place one foot after the other, escape her reflection and cross the lino to the stove, where the muck in a heap of cold saucepans spills in layers of burnt scabs and solidified mineral deposits, with a couple of stalactites dangling from one side of the hotplate. There is rubbish everywhere in various states of decay, some of it even in crazy stages of organisation (lots of crusts together, a heap of used teabags, stacked-up chicken bones). Anger shakes off her fear. How dare anyone live in such filth. How dare that woman not fear being found out. The whole place a risk to health, glib with madness, shamelessly nauseating. And the gorge does rise. She does gag. This is real. Smothering nose and mouth with a handkerchief, Olga is now determined to see it all, to confirm the correctness of her diagnosis – senile squalor syndrome – and the perfectly defensibly firm action she has taken: most of all in the interests of that pathetic creature herself, when it comes to the point.

In the murky corridor her feet stick to the carpet. She doesn't risk looking. The flies follow her. Pushing the first door wide open, she takes one look at the disgusting bed there, scrumpled sheets and heaped blankets. How brazen that woman must have become to so let herself go. To defy public standards. Sister Olga Ostrov, experienced nurse as she is, can testify categorically that she has never seen a slum to equal this. Fuelled by righteousness – her head balanced, precarious as porcelain and fragile with rage – she knows she need not sully her fingers in contact with a single article of that stinking clothing to make her case.

The bath and shower have remained unused for years, by the look of it. The place should be bulldozed down and buried. Serve the old witch right. No amount of work could make it habitable by any normal decent

love without hope

purchaser. Back in the kitchen again, Olga notices a scrap of paper pinned above the bench. A prescription. She reads Dr Parker's letterhead and the words *Ami tryptiline*. Then, ripping it from under the drawing-pin and stuffing it in her pocket, she storms back out into the blinding and virtuous freshness of open air.

The horses have gone.

The land breathes with contentment, weeds flowering along fence-lines where rusted relics of machinery sink into the soil: a harrow from the days of grain-growing, two bent lengths of guttering, stacks of wood, used bricks and roofing iron. The nurse has gone, slamming herself inside the car she parked outside the gate. She has driven off in a fury of dust.

The dust settles.

Gnats skate across a muddy pond. Near the gate stands a cluster of 44-gallon fuel drums, one with a hand-pump clipped to its rim. Although the wombat holes seem uninhabited, there is some awakening in the encroaching bush itself, trees have begun crowding for a closer view and leaning in. Shadows step around. Beyond the boundary the dense ramparts of eucalyptus and sprouting burrawangs are already alive with bird-winged insect-jointed spirits disturbing the leaf-mulch. Cliffs with their caves and mossy rocks echo a whipbird's cry.

The sky fills with spirits gathering to view the farm below, agitating the domesticated scene with speculations and swirling in their myriad inquisitiveness, elevated and murmurous, in the observance of a simple closure ritual – long awaited – the flourishing turf seen as a mere pall covering a recumbent and still-discernible female form. This gigantic female holds them, fluttering numerous as leaves in the forest, as a clan, crowded together and in no hurry: other intruders have not survived, but she has. They look down at her grass-clad form, half a kilometre long, and at the tiny squared irrelevance of house and yards set ceremonially on her head, at the horse trough held like a dish in her hand. They know with the knowing of two thousand generations – a vast and ever-tumbling avalanche of grief and laughter too cataclysmic to be confined – there is a heart here and the heart has not stopped beating, only half-buried by the soil and masquerading as bare peaceful folds of hillside.

Perhaps they sense, also, with the insight of belonging, an old woman who does not lie quiet under the exhaustion of age. Her spirit is among them. She is tomorrow's havoc.

Dr Archibald Parker, physician, attends to his routines. Whatever his regrets he cannot disown them. Yes, even setting aside the tangle of mistakes made since, he regrets that he did not stay in Europe when he undertook a hiking tour of the Pyrenees as a young man. And he regrets his subsequent enlistment in the International Brigade to fight the hopeless battle for Spanish democracy, regrets it not because he was wounded, nor because he has lost faith that the cause was just, but because experience teaches that there was never any point to the sacrifice. The world is corrupt. Those with

love without hope

power will, axiomatically, sacrifice the young when this power and their greed for it are threatened. The same holds true throughout the entire civilised world. And once the Vatican declared for Franco it should have been obvious that money would guarantee the enemy victory.

He unscrews the cap of a fresh bottle of Gilbey's.

John Cornford had charmed him. No doubt about that. With his earnest conviction, his Cambridge *savoir-faire*, his manly frankness. Not till Cornford stepped down from the platform to speak to him personally did he believe he would actually make the commitment and go. Though, having enlisted, the truth is that the whole catastrophe struck him as lacking in reality, right up till the moment when he sprawled in the dust clutching his leg and gritting his teeth, well aware that he mustn't expect others to put their lives at risk just because he was wounded. And the hopelessness of belief weighed on him during the hours of bleeding and the gradual mutation of the landscape to a rubbery parody of itself as his wandering sight faltered and he passed out.

Of course, someone did come to his rescue. The handsomest man he had ever seen propped up his head and fed him tiny trickles of delicious water and all around them the evening light congealed.

'From one colonial to another,' said his rescuer. 'You are Australian, I think?'

He'd nodded.

'I'm Argentinian, Carlos Anderführen. How do you do, comrade?'

'Thank you, Carlos.'

'Well, so it seems, we are the lucky ones. We should celebrate.'

'With what?'

'With our hearts.'

And only then did he notice a hideous bloodstain on his new friend's uniform still welling from the underarm down towards his belt.

'You should get that looked at,' he'd said.

'Really?'

'Yes. I speak as a medical student.'

'Then I shall do as you say,' Carlos Anderführen conceded and repositioned himself, squatting down so they could be more squarely face to face.

Doctor Parker pours a gin.

'So?' he'd said.

'Well, you're probably the nearest thing to a doctor this side of bleeding to death,' said his rescuer in perfect but accented English.

They had laughed together, then.

It makes him cry to think of. He was eighteen at the time.

Gail Savage calls on her husband at the village snack bar just to see if he needs anything done before she starts work on her good deed for the day. Habitually, she feels somehow in the wrong. She catches him in the shop window setting up a new display of properties for sale. And she smiles encouragingly because he is branching out into this new business and she hopes he will succeed. In fact, the land sales are already doing so well, he might soon be able to give up selling sandwiches and mugs of tea to concentrate on real estate fulltime. Perhaps then he can be happy. Which he certainly is not, as things stand. Also because she is frightened of him and she hopes to find a way out of this fear. She owes him so much, after all. He scowls at her through the glass. She mimes her offer, indicating her full shopping basket. He shakes his head before casting his eyes to heaven because it's obvious that if he wanted anything he could get it for himself, or eat his own stock.

So, at least, she has not needed to go in.

Gail proceeds past the Post Office, past the new doctor's surgery, to the CWA, in under the shadowy cypresses, where she fishes out the key and opens up. This is her favourite time of all because she can shut the door behind her, knowing nobody will come for at least another hour.

She stands a moment to recover her breath, confronted by rows of plastic stack chairs set out ready for a meeting, parallel shafts of light busy already with aerial dust motes and a couple of lost bees. She reads her own name in gold lettering up there on the framed honours board behind the lectern: *1981 Secretary*. That was a busy time. And she might have stayed on in the job if Russell hadn't done his block and accused her of neglecting her responsibilities. She passes among the phantoms of record attendances and supportive traditions, sensible discussions about parks and sewerage, feasts of cake and scones for receiving new clergymen, school fêtes, Anzac Day parades, and impassioned exchanges of recipes.

Having set out the necessary kitchen utensils she gets busy unpacking groceries. She flings cupboards open and

love without hope

chooses her meat trays and baking dishes. Here, fizzing with energy, she is incontestably mistress. The power of familiarity boosts her pretty breasts and straightens her shoulders. Her face already plumps out. She feels useful. Though there is one thing – one unanswered question – niggling her. She has not had space to attend to the implications till now, but here, in her domain, she fetches it out: should she include Mrs Shoddy in her numbers today? Rumours being mere rumours. She doesn't know. There has been no instruction from the committee. Rita Gibbons was supposed to report the treatment they had received at Mrs Shoddy's hands last Thursday. And here it is Monday without anything resolved.

It would seem a dreadful waste to cook six dinners if she need only deliver five. She meant to ask Rita at the supermarket. She forgot. Should she telephone now? Or simply cook enough to go round, though not so much that it can't be fitted on five plates – this being the advantage of shepherd's pie over flathead fillets? In other words, not to trouble anybody and just make the decision herself? Plus, Rita is always so definite and so critical of other people's hesitations. But, no. It offends her sense of duty and will never do.

Tying on an apron as she goes, Gail opens the door to the little office at the back. She knows the Gibbonses' number. Rita must decide. Meanwhile, she can begin with an easy mind and boil up some potatoes for the crust. The very instant she reaches for the phone, it rings. Guilty as ever, Gail leaps with shock. So that old black telephone rings and rings while she struggles to master her trepidation.

'Hello.'

'May I speak to Mrs Rita Gibbons?' (a man's voice). 'I'm ringing about the land.'

Gail glances up as if he might have arrived in person to take her by surprise, seeing only herself in a mirror advertising Nescafé.

'Rita's not here,' she observes her mouth mouthing.

'She's the president, so I understand?'

'Yes, but she won't arrive in for another hour.'

'Then I shall ring back.'

And he hangs up. Just like that. So fate seals her choice. Now she has a reason to ring Rita which will not look like dithering.

Mrs Shoddy has been shouting for an hour. One mightn't think she'd have the will or the strength, yet she shouts. Again a mocking chorus responds from the dormitory out there. But no one comes. Again she has been strapped up all night, not able to move. And she grieves for home. Her body's desperate needs torment her. Perpetually isolated on a stretcher in a tiny room so dim she can scarcely see, she lies in her own filth. And lying in her own filth, hearing the yells and whimpers of those lucky enough not to be in solitary confinement, Mrs Shoddy tells herself she was betrayed. I was betrayed by two trespassing women. But how could they bring themselves to dob me in? How could they fail to see that we women must stand together against the tyranny, the male trivia of possession and governance? But they did fail. And she had to run out at them, her blouse stained with a delicate stink of boiled vegetables, out from her mouldy stagnant kitchen into the roaring lion-mouthed sunshine. They backed away, too, taking the temptations they'd brought with them, skirts agitated and their painted mouths working at an apology, till car doors slammed shut on them, the motor rasped to life, and they escaped. Good riddance.

Am I to blame for not guessing they might have the power to take revenge on me? But they're nobodies. I had to make my point. Because why shouldn't I be left in peace to live the way I choose? What gives them the right to come prowling around, squinting in through the glass wherever they can find a crack between the curtains? I saw them treading my wallflower beds, young Gail Savage pointing to a squashed bucket under the thick grass and saying don't trip on that, Rita. Yes, I watched them tiptoe from the laundry to the livingroom window. They knew they weren't welcome. What right did they have?

Well, Mrs Shoddy knows the answer now. Though she never would have believed it possible, things came to a crisis with the ambulance arriving to cart her away. The horses watched her desperate hopeless struggles when they dragged her out, that's all, the horses and the spirits

love without hope

of the place. So, she conjures with a new idea. The Koories always claim to have special knowledge of the land, even hers, thanks to millennia of ownership beyond all reckoning. Certainly beyond our paltry concept of a past. So, have they kept watch on her family and the generations of horse-breakers, all these years? Have they been expecting this day even while watching her tyrant father nail sheets of corrugated metal to the roof to shut out the weather, watching her mother through the window stewing offal in the pot and watching Martin Shoddy arrive like Lord Byron on a motorbike, plus all the calamity of her own comings and goings? And might those old Koories move back now, in her absence – materialising from among the trees along the boundary fence – to storm her paddocks with slow-treading dingo-stealth? The latest tactic in a two hundred years' war? People subtle as shadows, their very feet remembering the land's loved body, despite finding it cropped back to the soil by horse teeth, its slopes and declivities, its waterways and nurturing secrets.

A shot of guilt surprises her trussed body. She asks herself if there might be some justice, then, in her removal from the farm. She is torn. She, Mrs Shoddy. Lorna Boswell, as was, daughter of Jack the Drunk. But even this is a certificate of her rights, here in the lunatic asylum. The grief of knowing unlocks her tongue.

'Help!' she calls.

The chorus calls back, 'Help, help!'

She cannot move. Home is where she must escape to. Her mind calls it into being so vividly the power of the place is all about her. She feels it. She can walk from room to room, handling the hairbrushes on her dressing table, standing before the mirror, pulling on her old jodhpurs and sorting through the clothes heap for a warm jumper. But what surprises her is a stranger arriving on the back porch and coming straight in through the open door. (Mrs Shoddy, stiff on a stretcher, squeezes her eyes as tightly shut as they can be.) Yes, a woman trespassing, already in among Mrs Shoddy's day-to-day things, a dim pale figure, transformed to shadow, outlined against the wash of window-light, crossing to the sink and then – pale again – passing into the corridor, only to rustle like a disapproving bird on spindly legs, shuffling its white plumage at what it finds in the bedroom. (Poor thing must want to sleep, Mrs Shoddy explains it to herself, she must want to sleep in my bed.) But no, next minute the shadowy intruder rushes back the way she came and out of the house altogether. Her whiteness explodes and dissolves into sunshine.

'Stop, thief! Thief!' Mrs Shoddy screams.

And she opens her eyes to find the giant from Jack and the Beanstalk pendent above her, his upside-down shaven head, his mammoth lips and grinning teeth. Blue collarless tunic buttoned at the neck. Vernon.

'Stop, thief?' he enquires with a touch of humour.

She feels like a child. She has a child's fear of giants. Her bed is a tree house in a falling tree, a sleeper on a train to nowhere, a raft adrift at sea. A cat has her in its claws. Is she the one who is upside down?

love without hope

'That woman in my house,' she gasps.

'How are you feeling?'

'Poking her nose in, whoever she is.'

His teeth are beautifully clean.

'Give us an hour or so and I shall be back to help you up.'

'She's been into my bedroom.'

'You know, Mrs Shoddy, when speaking about yourself, you can say *I*. That's not against the rules.'

'She. It's her.'

'Ha ha. I know this game. I've played this one before.'

'She wants something.'

'Breakfast, perhaps? All in good time. You'll probably need sponging first.'

Next thing, his face withdraws. He is gone. Before she has a chance to object. Because even an enemy is preferable to no one. 'Am I mad?' she whispers as the delirium of torments crowds in on her again with twitches and needlings, the aching blood static as a canal, her heart clenching and unclenching slow as a jellyfish, her brain a farmhouse filled with familiar light and smells, old comfortable corners, secretive cupboards, shadows reaching out to cradle her panic, loose windows and parting planks where flowers burst through the cracks. She cannot feel the straps that restrain her. Her little nerveless arms. Her nerveless chest and thighs. It frightens her to think about the pharaohs bound up in swaddling cloth, each one bandaged stiff, suffocating inside a mask, and fitted with a body-moulded coffin. Not for them the comfort of soil, the gentle rotting rupture till the delicate gelatinous flesh fell from their bones – no – like her, they were destined for a sterner fate, cured and straightened out, locked down in the prison of a permanent existence among divine beings half-animal, half-human, dog-nosed and vulture-winged and, in each form, enigmatic. She knows it. And how voice, vision, touch and taste must all be surrendered while the core comes to be drawn out as spirit, that irreclaimable spirit, eternally in search of lodgings under the cowl of alien winter darkness. She is among her horses down at the bottom of the home paddock. With them she looks up toward the house, her very own house, and sees a nurse emerge. A nurse! She needs a nurse. She needs help. Now is her chance, she should call out. But the small white figure already hurries to the gate – and, once there, sits herself inside a car, swings the wheel and glides, diminishing, away over the lip, on to the road – and out of sight. Mrs Shoddy watches the car dwindle. And the horses watch with her: they know something beyond human telling. There must be reasons why they cluster in this particular corner. Horses have accumulated a thousand years' experience of war, being whipped and goaded to gallop full tilt into disasters where they had no will to go. They understand what it is to hold back their spooky temptations to chaos, checked at the brink, to expel fear and let ferocity take its place, hurling themselves headlong, manes flying, tails streaming, at an enemy of armaments, of bristling steel formations, while blood runs down

love without hope

their flanks and foam flakes off them in the wind of their abandon. Such needs have shaped them and shaped the normal morning ritual of munching grass, too, and shaped their reasons for assembling round her in placid companionable alertness.

Even her father admired her knack with horses. So much so that he complained about the expense of sending her to boarding school to learn Latin when all she did was moon over her pony during the exams and go copying the raciest of the mistresses (the one with a sports car) once she got home. But that was before Alzheimer's struck him down and she watched unmawkish angers show till, the more helpless his mind, the more furiously he'd grind his teeth and mutter. She watched his eyes fill with virgin tears and his conversation change till he began circumventing such nouns as he could not recall, wandering across the barren territory of abstraction ('when... that fellow who used to live across the road brought me the... the very thing I needed for my ... he only came to look *you* over, you know that?'), more and more often losing his way before being struck down by a complete blank. Anyway, that particular storm never broke, the fellow he referred to was nothing but a lout whose most exacting intellectual achievement was to read the rain gauge of a morning and record the fractions of an inch in the notebook provided in a covered tin.

Martin, when Martin came along, took one look at the wreck of Father and dismissed him as irrelevant.

'Lorna suspects,' he nudged the old man, 'you want her to marry your neighbour so she can spend a happy lifetime with him. Well, I've knocked around a fair bit, surviving and getting to understand people, and you can take my word for it, that fellow's an oaf.' She remembers so well. And her father's face going purple with blocked up rage. And Martin explaining, 'Well, when I say I've knocked around I mean I've spent time pondering the nature of substance and illusion. And perhaps you'll be good enough to assure your delightful daughter that she needn't keep pulling faces at me. I'm not taking advantage of your forgetting. It's just that I don't give a damn what you think of me. So we shall have something in common.'

Maybe she had no right to (nor any rights over) a fiery creature like Martin. Who knows? Martin had been lent, in a manner of speaking, lent to her for a limited period only. He merely showed up, materialising from some element not her own. Though come to think of it, neither of her cousins, Angus and Lachlan, nor any of the larrikins in the district, were born to be as they had become. This had probably been the case with her father as well, but cracks appeared once the mask slipped, and his certainties dropped off chunk by chunk till he was left soft-centred and disarmed. So it all seemed to have been for nothing, that bluster.

Men construct themselves, her unfettered intelligence tells itself, father to son, brother to brother, they pass on a hand-me-down of *acceptability,* so then all the rest can be added as trimmings. Once a teenage lad gets the hang of the main game he chooses from a warehouse of possibilities – swearing, facial hair, rolled-up sleeves, elastic-sided boots, swagger, drawling voice – and therefore remains uncertain about them for the rest of his life.

Martin was not self-made in this sense. He had a way with women that was altogether natural. Otherwise he showed scarcely a trace of acceptability. His skill as a lover was too intense for the mere performance of virility. Indeed, he lost himself in such swooning savage surrender, sometimes lasting hours, she discovered she could throw her body at his and exhaust herself there. Long gone the time when she thought every man grunted at the beastly labour of sex.

As for talk, he could talk a hole in your hat. Ideas tumbled out. He seemed able to draw them down from some inexhaustible reservoir of the collective. And then let them go. He had that gift. The very next day, or even after a matter of hours, he would come up with something else. Brash and careless of people's feelings, he loved contradictions. The last time he walked out and abandoned her without a word, Lorna had no one to turn to.

Perhaps it was inevitable that she would end like this. Strapped to a creaky stretcher.

She lies passive while the staff arrive to assess her needs, switch on a light and look her over, then leave, switching the dark back on, abandoning her to the vortex of her hopeless outrage, her thunderous isolation in impotence. She blames herself for not calming her voice or choosing the right words to say thank you (for imprisoning me), thank you (for torturing me with immobility), and thank you (for humiliation piled upon humiliation). This, then, is the result of her loving fidelity all those years ago, her rapture, her headstrong abandonment in the arms of the only lover she'd known. He left. And he left her incapable of loving again. Otherwise, would she be abandoned and helpless now? She would not. If Martin had stayed he would have fought the bushfire and saved her from what Dr Parker diagnosed as clinical depression. More. Martin would have sent those women packing with their charity food undelivered, he would have barred the gate and thrashed any Vernon-type paramedic daring to step on to his land. So, Lorna Shoddy reviews her life, a life she once lived without knowing it, a life of capable horse-handling, during which she thought herself sufficient in management, when really she was teetering on eggshells. In the silence of despair the one thing she is most afraid of is losing him.

'Are you dead?' her mind cries out to her lover.

'What do you wish to hear?' she hears him reply.

And his voice gets the blood zinging through her exhausted body.

'I want you to explain why you went,' she says, collecting herself, 'why you just walked away, without a word.'

'I set out to find something new. That's all.'

'*I* was not new?'

love without hope

'In search of some game I could engage in. To test my skill.'

'But why?'

'To stay young.'

'Are you dead?' she cries while he stands invisibly before her.

'What I found was ... something you would not believe.'

'So you are a success? I hear it in your voice. You are a success without me.'

'I am a failure. Huge. You would despise me.'

'How will you ever know unless you tell me?'

The door opens. A deluge of light tumbles in. Mrs Shoddy cannot move her hands to shield her eyes. And she dare not shut them now Vernon has come. She suffers the glare like a kick in the head. His ogre's silhouette bleeds into its halo, printed on water-spoiled paper. She can smell him, some trace of deodorant faintly and repulsively feminine. Legs apart, hands on hips, he contemplates her misery. Martin's voice has gone.

As her eyes grow used to the element she has them for, she sees past him. In the transparency of an institutional dormitory, a place of so many beds she cannot calculate, there are other figures walking between the rows, passing and repassing: women, yes. She sees their breasts in brown uniforms, their once-proud and arching pelvises, their round soft worn-down heels. All ordinary. But their heads are monstrous, encased in padded helmets, helmets made (she now sees) of rope, and right then one bounces against the wall. Like combatants in some unimagined arena of war they slouch about their business. Yet she sees nothing of triumph in this helmet-wearing. Nothing of combat, nor the delirium of risk that speeds the blood. They wear them like teapots wear tea-cosies, humbly and with the shame of accidental crookedness.

Vernon is above her, upon her, leaning into her, and Mrs Shoddy knows he believes he is welcome. Her intuition tells her that he is in this job without the faintest comprehension of how his patients might see him. She's already sure he goes home to his partner of whatever sex or age and flops in an armchair, uttering the gratified noises of bulk, growling and explaining that: At least I am there for them, so they can have the comfort of knowing they are not abandoned or alone or without help. I am always attentive and caring. And doubtless, she thinks, his partner ministers to him the way he wants and says: Of course, darling, of course you are, you're a wonderful person, they should count themselves lucky, those lunatics, you're more than they deserve and I should know. Mrs Shoddy can tell because he still carries with him that stroked air of an appreciated person. And the armour of it is impermeable. He bends to unbuckle her straps. And in these moments of expectation she does find the words she wants.

'Thank you,' she whispers.

One after another he yanks at the buckles, each one pinching harder during the moment before release. Then

love without hope

she is free to stand. But she cannot. What's worse, her arms are still bound by that hideous garment they put her in. He reaches out imperiously, helping her – yanking her upright, balancing her on feet grown too small – demanding to know whether or not she is ready to be calm, ready to be set free (within the confines of these barred windows and shut doors) and whether she can be trusted not to injure others or set them off, because *setting them off* is the worst offence of all.

'My horses,' she gasps, now she knows she was wrong and he is here to help.

But he drops her in the corner where she can think again. Roughly, he picks up the soiled bed, a frame with a woven wicker pallet for lying on, and its flimsiness in his massive hand is a dismissal. He turns, the breadth of his calm back all she can see, to walk away. Out through the door. Leaves her, so that even she, even in her state of bewilderment and confusion, cannot misunderstand – he has been trained to give clear messages – that she has done the wrong thing mentioning her horses and that she had better slump there in discomfort a while longer to reconsider her responsibilities to the smooth running of this institution where she is fortunate to have been granted a place. Swishing the soiled bed through before him and casting it to one side on the floor, he closes the door. The little dangling brass cover of the peephole (on the outside, of course) jingles as it swings down over the only lens of daylight left. She last sees it as a new moon.

She does not cry out. She knows better. The misery goes beyond utterance. The tiny core of her existence is buried beneath unfeeling hillsides. She must abandon her body altogether, brittle diminished little object that it has become. Yet, Mrs Shoddy feels the first awakening of a power in herself. Some sound – like the shuddering enormity of an organ note – reaches her through a floor soaked in the piss and tears of the demented. She understands with fracturable transparency where she is.

She is not insane.

She understands she has been betrayed and judged, she has been the victim of contempt – contempt so unimaginably virulent they'll do this to her rather than tolerate letting her live on in her own way, minding her business and troubling no one. She understands that the cowardice of her persecutors is so craven they haven't the grace to kill her outright nor the intelligence to doubt their own grounds for belief. For an hour or two she dwells on their poverty of spirit. How strangled the imagination would need to have become not to recognise the brutality, not recognise the monumental vulgarity of what they are doing to her. Had it been worse for people thrust into gas chambers? How? Yet her persecutors would surely recoil in shock from any such comparison. That would be too violent a rupture of the very values, the decency and cleanliness, they delude themselves they can uphold by keeping her here. She knows she has been shut away so she will not disrupt the conformity of others, out there where she used to

love without hope

live, nor offend their orderly blunted conventions. Their marshmallow morality. Their pliant, even pious, complicity in a suffocating society no better than a soapie.

She feels revived already.

She insists on her command of the rules of logic having, after all, read *Beyond Good and Evil* (mostly in English, but a little, to pay herself credit, in German too). This is what she sees before her, this vivid logic, sees it in the gloom created by solid wooden shutters shutting out the windows, the solid wooden door being shut, the peephole covered and herself in a tiny but barely visible room. At last she has an inkling of what Nietzsche called the will to power. But how did he ever guess? The Hero, as she remembers it, must affirm life in the face of meaninglessness. Yes, meaninglessness: not actual death. That's what so particularly speaks to her now.

She suspects Vernon of lurking outside the door, listening for her cries. Crying out hasn't helped persuade him to release her yet. And if she does he will know she is suffering. No, she gets a grip: crying merely surrenders power to him and he loves his power. He will seize it where he can and never give it back. Growing bigger and bigger, he will leave her there caged like a dangerous beast for months or years while she shrivels to a shadow.

Since Martin left, the film has spooled out of control, streaming through the sprockets of her loneliness, events crowding so quickly she has no chance to reflect on them, all she can do is accept that normal experience –

whatever *normal* might mean – is passing her by. Even to the fact that she had no children.

Well, the lack of children was never more felt than now.

So, how is she to deal with the urgent truth that her horses need someone (someone who knows how to do it) to switch on the pump to fill their troughs during her absence, to let them into the ten-acre paddock for fresh grass? Another couple of days and the poor dears will be in trouble. How can she explain in such a place to such people? Unless they volunteer to listen? The best she can suggest is producing the behaviour they want. Yes, till they untie this hideous immobilising garment. Till they let her out into a space where she might encounter someone able and willing to understand, someone she can tell, someone she can persuade to her cause, even someone who might telephone her one surviving friend in the village, Elsie Southwell, whom she has neglected in recent years, unwisely neglected, but who knew her before the fire when she was robust and cheerful, who will not bear grudges and who has a car for driving out to the farm. She has scarcely given Elsie a thought till now, but Elsie would do it. And only need be asked. And after tending the horses' requirements – who knows? – she might be willing to track Martin down.

Mrs Shoddy tries standing by herself, now she's off the bed and no longer strapped to it, and totters, canting against the wall. But she will not weep. Soon the nurses will come to feed her – and this time she will be more

love without hope

sensible, she will thank them and accept the pap they spoon between her lips, supping, tasting, savouring. She will encourage them to feel grateful to her for believing they are appreciated. Then she will beg them, calmly beg them, to release her arms so she can deal with the pins-and-needles, so she can shield her eyes and massage her weary old flesh back to life. They need never know how much is necessity and how much is an act. Such creatures would not suspect themselves of being outwitted. Not here. She is composed. She is ready.

No one comes.

'What land?' Rita Gibbons demands to be told.

'He didn't say,' says Gail, oven muffs protecting her hands as she reaches out to placate the old woman.

'But who was he?'

'He didn't say,' Gail says helplessly.

Rita inspects the mashed potato set ready in a bowl and the mince in the casserole dish beside it.

'He must have left a number.'

'No,' Gail confesses. And then she adds, 'But he said he's going to ring back.'

love without hope

'You mean to stand there, Gail Savage, and tell me you don't know *anything*?'

'It was a long-distance call,' Gail remembers helpfully.

Martin neither denied his Aboriginal grandmother nor claimed her. The same with the law of the Koorie people. Without understanding it or living under it he left room for respect: room created by his extremely wary endorsement of the penal code brought by the British. The translucent grey shadows modelling his white skin were the only visible inheritance Martin had from that side of his ancestry. But when he told Lorna about this grandmother (and she suspected it might be a somewhat boastful alliance with the two thousand generations of Koories who had lived on her

love without hope

land) she said: Who could care? And added, turning his own scorn for ancestry against him: Blood is blood and necessary for life, that's all. And she'd meant it, as she enlarged her point: *Where* it comes from is neither here nor there – as for me, I don't give a fig for my forebears. She'd challenged him gaily: So why should I bother about yours? And she'd watched him absorb the comfort of this as well as the dismissal. Being Martin, his lips had twisted sardonically: You might at least find it interesting as a connection, he'd said. Oh, connections! she'd laughed. You're the one to talk!

Yet, maybe Martin knew – through the knowledge held and hived in that particle of blood – what loss had been suffered. He had never needed persuading that ordinary and otherwise well-meaning people are capable of killing. And will. He warned her, too, but she did not believe. Not at the time. But she now suspected this particle of Aboriginal blood of freeing him to pursue his intuitions, freeing him from respectability. Was that too fanciful?

She, by contrast, has had to stumble upon her own innocence, she who never encouraged the habit of thinking herself innocent. But the reason why she's crying is because the pain grows unbearable as her present reality crashes through the pretence that she can escape into a world of the mind. The body's rampant needs have her in their pincers. So, when the door opens and a nurse almost as gigantic as Vernon comes in, a woman with cropped hair and a man's face, a woman grim as a crumbling cliff, Mrs Shoddy forgets her resolutions and her reason.

The room is a chaos of reflected daylight glaring on tin plate covers, a sickle of light along the spoon edge, a glitter in the nurse's eye, a sinister curl of steam, the mirror-bright oblong of floor and her own vain sobs and screams as she spits out the food she is fed. She writhes against restraint. That's when she glimpses another female patient, a mere ghost, a woman wearing the rope helmet of her disgrace, who glances in, pauses and glances again with liquid black eyes set in a kindly round face, a woman whose cheeks have known laughter and whose skin is so brown as to be almost black.

The nurse, missing nothing, checks back over her shoulder.

'That's enough staring, Julie,' she warns.

As Julie shuffles away her weighted head tilts to one side in a gesture of compassion, which Mrs Shoddy reads with piercing clarity. So, it *is* possible to survive this place somehow intact! She finds she has swallowed a morsel of the pap.

'Good,' exclaims the nurse, surprised. 'Now another spoon.'

Suddenly what was insurmountably difficult is so easy as not to be noticed. The food, incredibly, tastes of food. Mrs Shoddy waggles her helpless unseen fingers.

'Good,' says the nurse again and her mannish face smiles, momentarily revealing a kindly person who has known too much injury to forget or forgive.

love without hope

The tears come unbidden. Yet Mrs Shoddy manages to stay calm, just as she promised herself she would.

'Pins and needles,' she pleads.

'Well, dear,' says the nurse, her voice a melody, 'you've been put in that thing to prevent you doing yourself an injury. It's called a camisole.'

Mrs Shoddy is on the verge of plunging into anger and screeching: It's a bloody *straitjacket*, you don't fool me! But she holds back. She is learning. The one thing she must remember is to suppress her fears and avoid shouting about her horses, or mentioning the bushfire, or that her family doctor (even through his gin fog) told her the bitter truth. This is not a person who will help with the horses. Even so, one step at a time, this *may* be a person who can restore the use of her arms. That at least.

'I won't hurt myself,' she promises meekly.

'Shall I write a note on your report for Vernon to consider?'

Mrs Shoddy sees into the soul of the woman leaning over her, a woman who perhaps always longed to be delicate and feminine and insipid – and still might be, within that massive frame. It gives her a glimpse of herself too: feeling her heart thud and the minutes thunder past while she tarries here, caught up in the terror of an avalanche, boulders and bouncing rocks surging down a vast slope, seeing her sanity stand as a tiny figure paralysed with fright . . . and immune only if she remains on that very spot without flinching.

'I don't see why we shouldn't give it a go,' the nurse

sizes her up, assessing a risk in the tremendous silence of admitted morning light, and wavering between her personalities.

'You're so kind.'

Next thing, it's done. The tapes have been untied, her crossed arms slump at her sides, the straitjacket is revealed in its demonic simplicity, a mere rag of canvas, empty sleeves and a fold-over top. Mrs Shoddy, shaky and tottering, yet manages a comment.

'It's just a camisole,' she admits, 'after all.'

The avalanche, having passed, can still be heard crashing down into some remote and thickly forested valley, some cleft that swallows everything, rocks, rubble, fear and the mythic wind that travels with it.

'Will you finish your food now? Well done.'

The terrible blood pushes back into her veins. Tears spring to her eyes like the thrust of hot barbed-wire as life returns. She shudders violently. She cannot feel her rattling fingers, though she believes she will. Sometime soon. They must still be down there, the useless things. Mrs Shoddy concentrates: the main thing is to keep Vernon out of it. She must always be alert to this, the first rule of survival. Munching slops and struggling to produce from her fatigue the shapes and prattle of satisfaction. So, food becomes her next success. And she has finished it. What's more, she has found her fingers and holds the spoon for herself, despite so great a trembling that she smears her cheeks with gravy. She feels her new friend leaning close to warm her.

'Do you think you can stand?'

love without hope

She does. But she cannot. Not at the first try, anyway. The nurse helps. So, now Mrs Shoddy finds herself borne up by the inexhaustible strength of someone twice her size, someone willing to serve her, with a force like a rising wave at sea. Even despite the towering grief of this place, she feels a tremor of hope. A voice speaks right into her ear.

'My name is Felicity.'

'Happiness,' Mrs Shoddy translates abstractedly, even while considering fate cruel to saddle so feminine a name with such shoulders and a face hacked from a log with an adze.

'How did you know that?'

Mrs Shoddy simply sighs because she will not be believed.

'How did you know that?' the nurse's amazement persists.

'I guessed,' she mumbles.

'You're something of a surprise package, aren't you? Now, try taking a step forward. I'll hold your arms. I won't let you fall.'

(Not like your friend Vernon who dropped me in the corner. And I shall never forget, even when I get out of here.)

'Look,' says Mrs Shoddy, seeing the woman she'd noticed earlier. She waves a few uncoordinated fingers. And the tea-cosy solemnly returns her gaze.

'Say hello to Julie,' the nurse suggests.

'Hello, Julie.'

'Hello.'

'That's the ticket. We're doing fine.'

'There's angels here,' Julie whispers.

'Now then, Julie,' Nurse Felicity invites a retraction.

'And demons,' Julie puts in hastily while she still has the chance.

Mrs Shoddy won't comment for fear of compromising herself because she is a Christian and because she believes in the Devil too, which is quite out of fashion, as she knows. But Julie has already seen, anyway. At the far end of the dormitory Vernon approaches, an ice-breaker cracking and fracturing the morning as he pushes it before him, forcing it to tilt and buckle on either side.

'Now we must walk back in,' says Nurse Felicity with her beautiful distinctness, 'because I don't have the authority to let you sleep out here with the good girls. Round we go.'

'Who's she?' asks Julie, not wanting to be shut out.

'This is Lorna,' says the nurse's back.

They are already in the dark room where there is no chair to sit on, only a black pot against one wall.

'That's for your night soil, now you're out of the restraint.'

'Oh?'

'I can't bring you any furniture. It's against the rules, because you could hurt yourself.'

'I am already hurt,' Mrs Shoddy dares answer, staggering now, with her wings broken and propping her tremulous body against the wall.

love without hope

'Well, I won't put the camisole on you again. I shall speak to Vernon about that, since he's here. I shall just leave you. I have my rounds to do.' She deftly lets herself out. 'I'm very pleased with you,' she sings as the door closes.

Mrs Shoddy has already glimpsed a speeding Vernon about to collide with a momentarily defiant Nurse Felicity. She hears nothing of what they say through the thick door.

'So, she's very pleased with you?' Martin comments promptly.

'Only because I betrayed my horses.'

'There's plenty of feed in that paddock, you know.'

She doesn't think this warrants an answer because he must realise she is talking about love. She can't stand up a moment longer, so she sinks. She crouches in her corner, feeling the accumulated cold of that cold stone bunker.

'I made a lot of money,' Martin offers eventually.

'But I thought you said you are a failure?'

'Same thing.'

Not a word about why he never shared this money, nor even came to rescue her from loneliness. Not a word of regret. And certainly nothing about how he'd had to flee some country or other to avoid jail. Yet she knows this, in a flash: she hears it in his voice, a voice so palpable she feels it vibrate in her flesh, this clever voice, lazy and calm and calmly mocking, the voice of a sensualist, a lover. Her lover. All that matters is finding him. Or being found by him. Whichever. All that matters is the chance to escape. And, for a start, she has lured him to her. Ah, yes, at long last. He is, after all, only a man. More like the others, maybe, than she used to think. More like her own father, even. And hadn't she watched the old man grow decrepit and forgetful when his mind began going and he took to weeping in a helpless rage against helplessness, his impotence circling on itself and finding no escape into even the simplest logical connection by which he might haul himself out of the pit that he knew was bottomless with death. Oh yes, and then she saw it: her own father (the very pattern and archetype of a man) had made it all up. The business of being a man and being in charge.

So what if Martin was not such an exception? What if he, too, had *chosen* how he would be, as he starved the fat from his body and worked what was left to the hardness of a steel spring, rather than simply being what he was? Impossible. Why? Because the difference was that his own mind amused him and he was never afraid to admit his limits. And never afraid of the unknown. When he seized on knowledge it was as if he had a right to it, like common land, and he set his herd of questions to graze where they chose. She saw these questions, looming shadowy unsleeping shapes, chanced upon by night, more like passive mastodons than cattle, monumental with innocence.

So why should she be surprised if he had made money? Hadn't he always said money is no more substantial than air? Why should she doubt that he had written a book, or that he might have begun it by standing in some Asian temple with winged roofs – wasn't it just like him to pause with pad and pencil and write *travel is simple, you need less money to live here than at home, all you need is the will to let go of safety* – choosing his words to show the reader (her) the ceiling as he saw it, with two gilded dragons coiled among painted flowers, and the agents of an alien state striding across the wooden floor to arrest him? Anyway, it's what she imagines. And it's how she comforts herself.

So now she waits for him to ask about her and the life she has led since he left, about the horses they had raised together, horses he had helped break in and train. But his silence on the subject becomes forbiddingly courteous. Apparently he already knows too much to put her on the spot. After all, hadn't he and she shared every task and every setback? Hadn't they laughed over the same eighteenth century satires, the same twentieth century simplicities of Daffy Duck and Buster Keaton? Hadn't they argued the toss about Übermensch and gloried in the Victory at Stalingrad? Hadn't they discovered Schubert's D958 piano sonata together? Hadn't they zoomed around the big dipper like a couple of kids and then gone home to tackle the drought? Didn't they always discuss the livestock breeding? So, his reticence clearly indicates his respect for her, his willingness to listen, but also his tact.

'Had I taken myself captive already?' she cuts in on

the pain this hesitancy of his causes her. 'Even before the Master in Lunacy got hold of me?'

'You tell me.'

'One thing,' she counters. 'After you left me I used to pin notes to the trees for you to read, just in case you might come lurking around again.'

'So you never changed?'

'I changed so much you would not know me. The horses are the only ones who don't see it. While you were travelling the world and feeling so clever I went down. Steeply down. And what terrifies me here is that they talk about psycho-surgery in front of me, as if I won't understand what this means. Why don't they just kill me? That would be simplest.'

Oh, but the truth is that she is talking to herself. As Mrs Shoddy is all too painfully aware, she knows nothing of Martin's life. After he left he never wrote. Not once.

The door opens. And it is still day. The light of afternoon as brilliant as morning. All that has changed is the angle from which it slants through a gallery of barred windows in among the dull metal legs of more beds per row than she can estimate, creating a complex pattern of shadows on the floor. Flying in on this magic carpet of light the giant Vernon advances a leer in her direction. The leer being both a question and a challenge. So, he blames her already. He knows she has won a victory over Felicity and he wants her to know she won't win over him.

love without hope

'I hear complimentary news about you, Lorna,' says Vernon reassuringly, while she is amazed by his thick neck and wide jaws. 'Well, tonight we shall let you choose. You can choose between your bed or your camisole. Either you'll have both or neither. There's a step up for you. The rules allow for a choice. Of course, I'm answerable to Mr Radcliffe and he'll need to give the nod. Still, I can't see him withholding approval. So, you'll let me know which it's to be, won't you?'

Gail Savage is soothed on her way back into town by knowing she has done her best. After all, she has never been much at home with appreciation (even as a child her freckles and prominent teeth disqualified her from all but the attentions of an uncle . . . and that turned out to be nasty), nor does she really expect it. Married at seventeen, for a start.

Driving, she negotiates the rutted road. The silence of her thoughts isolates her, despite having Rita there in the passenger seat atop a swaying mound of breasts.

'Well,' Rita concludes while checking her beautifully

love without hope

filled-out Discharge Book – she has a touch, when it comes to bookwork, no doubt about that – 'so we are left with one portion of everything wasted.' Nagged as she is by the usual imminent headache, she snaps the cover shut.

Gail, defending herself and, in part, defending the missing Mrs Shoddy, steers to avoid a pothole: 'I suppose she couldn't help it.'

'I'm notin' everythin' down in my records as I go.'

The corroding gloom eats into Gail's buoyancy. Is she to be blamed that she cooked too much, or that the portions of shepherd's pie could not be equalised because Rita herself hadn't been told whether or not anybody would be home when they got there? Surely, this wouldn't be fair?

'She'd gone.'

'Or been took,' Rita cavils ominously.

'How do you mean?'

'Spirited.'

'Away?'

'Altogether.'

'Who by?'

'Aha!'

Gone is Gail's pleasant memory of the others: Gerry Boyd rubbing his gnarled knuckles and warily watching Rita with his little chipped glass eyes while declaring her meal the best he ever had, Grannie Osborne kissing them both and calling them angels, Mrs Colonel Brady allowing them credit for punctuality, at least. All pushed out of mind by this business of Mrs Shoddy's empty house, a house open to whoever might walk in.

'I don't like the look of it,' Gail offers as an opening.

But Rita, though prepared to listen to gossip, is really a specialist in her own interests. For all the dignity of her family, she is one of those people whose intellectual enquiry into their own feelings and memories is too demanding for them to acquire much in the way of other knowledge ('she said and I said and I remember how last time my Arthur agreed to go and chop the head off one of their cockerels though they had the nerve to say he couldn't use their axe and he'd have to come back over the road to fetch his own well I said to him and if only he'd listen to me more often he'd be that much better off I said you're the shire clerk no less as he *was* in those days so never mind about hurting anybody's feelings supposing they have feelings that can be hurt . . .' and so on, 'but he never . . .' and so on). The one thing Rita does respect is a secret. And even when she doesn't have one up her sleeve she likes it to be thought that she has.

'There are some who know more than they're telling,' she intimates darkly, placing a finger against the side of her nose.

Gail finds this gesture irritating, if not actually distressful. She doesn't quite understand what it signifies. In her family, people didn't know you could get away with that kind of thing. Making an inspired effort, she hazards a guess.

'Would you be speaking of the man who rang?'

love without hope

'He turns out to be someone very important, so I hear tell. The only wonder to me is that he ever heard of any individual called Shoddy.'

The car bounces over the ruts towards town. Empty dishes rattle in the basket, the smell of congealing shepherd's pie leftovers does not entice. Gail – with the washing-up to look forward to, plus cleaning the kitchen, those jobs that no one takes into account – has had enough.

'I didn't mean to intrude,' she objects in a huff.

But her companion, picking a ginger hair from Gail's shoulder and then brushing the spot with wrinkled fingertips, is sufficiently put out by the indelicacy not to mind a rift between them.

'I wonder,' she wonders out loud, 'what that Olga was doing, walking into your husband's office? I saw her with my own two eyes. Don't tell me *she* has property! I thought they were supposed to be underpaid . . .'

This leaves poor Gail with nothing to say. It touches a nerve because the same question – having lodged itself in her mind two hours previously – has proved a stumbling block to every explanation she brings to bear on it, even the implausible ones.

'. . . nurses,' Rita Gibbons elaborates, to nail home her point.

'I suppose someone must have taken Mrs Shoddy away.'

'Committed her,' the older woman dares face the possibility.

'Poor little thing.'

'Not if she's mad.'

'How can anyone be sure? But she is lonely all right.'

'I used to know her father. Drinkin' man, not to put too fine a point on it. My Arthur couldn't stand a bar of him. As for herself... well, she got bad when she got thin.' Rita's tapping finger on her handbag confirms it. 'What more can you say?'

Though, for her part, Gail prefers to give the benefit. 'Well...'

'You were there on Thursday. You saw the way she went for us. Like a little rat she was, all teeth and whiskers. Chasing us off, as if we come asking for something. As if *we're* the ones wantin' a favour. The cheek! Us, taking her good wholesome food, who's beyond preparin' any such thing for herself.'

'Suppose she simply went out? I mean, walked? Not knowing where she was, nor where she was headed? Just walked because nobody stopped her? I mean, what if she's in the bush right now and not a single soul realising she's gone at all? Excepting us, that is? What if she's injured and lying helpless in some gully?'

'Oh yes, and what if she's been nailed up on a cross! You let your imagination run away, if you ask me, Gail. Just like your mother used to. You're all too fond of fancy ideas. She's been took, that's what. Simple. Sad though it is.'

The car lurches round a bend, narrowly missing an oncoming truck, and plunges into the swirl of its passing.

love without hope

'Well, I shall have it out when I see Olga.'

'You do that,' the older woman agrees with satisfaction, because this kind of hare-brained driving, enough to get them both killed, is proof of the complaint she lodged with the committee only last week, a complaint she insisted on seeing written into the minutes.

'Olga will know, if anybody does.'

Crossly, they bounce along, side by side. The senior lady sharpens her critical concentration on details, a whole catalogue of dissatisfactions in the making, critical of the corrugated road itself, her momentary triumph fading into a distinctly queasy feeling of the unwilling traveller being jolted worse than is good for a body. And the more she gives thought to the subject, the more she's put out by the mention of that phone call. Not just because she had to explain herself to Gail, after a fashion, but because any such call was made in the first place. What on earth had possessed Russell Savage to give anyone *her* number at the CWA? Let alone disowning his part in the process? She cannot fathom it. Not at all. Nor the notion that it 'might be made worth her while'. How might it? She resents being put in a position of giving her word to mention nothing to Gail – his wife, for crying out loud! – nor her own Arthur, for that matter. Well, she gave His Nibs forty-eight hours, that's what. 'Very well,' she'd told the telephone, 'tell me what you're talking about by Thursday morning or I shall be making enquiries . . . as to why my good name has been used,' she'd explained, 'without my permission.'

The one thing she dreaded was that the whole town might hear. Because goodness knows what rumours that would set going.

'A penny for your thoughts,' says Gail.

But she's the last one to trust! You could scarcely call Gail Savage discreet! Never a malicious girl. No, you couldn't lay that at her door. Nonetheless she's one of that younger set who run off at the mouth at the least opportunity, her very goodheartedness being her weakness.

'I can't for the life of me imagine,' says Rita tartly, 'why Olga couldn't have told us straight out and saved us the journey.'

'She must have known,' the driver agrees with caution.

Mrs Gibbons nods meaningfully at the road, as if to say: Keep your eye on the job, if you don't mind! But she purses her lips and holds her counsel. However long it takes, she is determined to remain silent until safely delivered at her front gate. She gives her diamond ring a good twisting.

Russell Savage brushes his wife aside impatiently. What is she prattling about? He doesn't even notice her high colour as he crams the last of the sandwiches into his mouth.

'Olga?' he boggles and keeps her waiting till he has swallowed the lot. 'Olga? Well, what do you think? She came in to pester me about that block of land she wants on the Woodland Estate.' He waves his free hand in the direction of a wall display of properties for sale. 'The best way of affording it, I told her, is to have the money.'

Gail watches him, surprised to see him flailing

around. He never normally uses his hands to help him talk.

'What does she think I'm running here?' he asks without inviting an answer. 'A charity?'

'I shouldn't have thought a patch of land out that way would cost much,' she dares take it further.

'No more it does. Still, she's a little matter of eight thousand short.'

He snorts and punishes his mouth with a paper napkin.

'If I say so myself,' he supplies to fill the silence between them, 'I make a corker of a sandwich.'

'I almost brought you a helping of shepherd's pie,' she confesses.

'I love shepherd's pie.'

But he seems too eager and her suspicions are aroused.

'That's why I thought it might be best for dinner tonight,' she says, to keep him talking.

'I'll go along with that.'

'You don't mind if it's leftovers?'

'Nup,' he sniffs, thinking it over, even so, and adding cannily, 'Who died then?'

'Mrs Shoddy got taken away. Or, at least, that's what we have to suppose. Her house is still open and birds picking over the rubbish in the kitchen.'

He looks up at her with such sudden interest she cannot account for it. The office chair squeals. His beefy hand snatches up the empty paper bag and crushes it to

love without hope

a small greasy ball. His eyes take her in, as if to engulf her. She steps back to be out of reach.

'You never saw such a sight,' she explains.

He rises to his feet with ominous deliberation.

'And Mother Gibbons was with you in the car,' he states.

'Why?'

'Just asking.'

But he wasn't.

'Of course. She always comes along.'

'You know something? You've done me a favour,' he concedes, grimacing as he catches the gratitude in her glance.

'Or, I *think* you have,' he takes it back. 'I'll know for sure when I ring the shire manager.'

When Mrs Shoddy wakes she has no idea of the time, nor why her cell door stands wide open. Stiff from sleeping on the floor, she bundles up her weak flesh and helps herself to her feet by clawing at the shiny walls, glad, at least, to have the use of her hands. She approaches the doorway to the big empty dormitory. Two junior nurses fetch folded nighties from huge white wardrobes and distribute them, one on the foot of each bed. They go about their work in silence, breasting the dauntingly bright sunlight.

Supported by the doorjamb, Mrs Shoddy stands at the

love without hope

brink of a chasm. The brink of an abyss of sorrow. She totters against vertigo, bracing herself lest she fall. Especially because the dormitory looks so invitingly like an escape. Would these busy young women even notice her if she slipped out? Seen through the long windows the garden looks bright and welcoming. And with bare feet she could be silent as a ghost. She could be out there in a jiffy. But she remembers the nighttime screams. Screams from women in these beds. Screams that emerge from the labyrinth of forgotten nameless faces of mothers and despots, leaving her lopsided upon waking and convinced illnesses are busy tugging at her body, her blind staring into the dark of the sealed-off room she's shut in.

Mrs Shoddy calculates the distance. Wonky though she is, she could surely be out and away in a minute. But, like a hand on her chest, something stops her. And she knows. It's the pain of so many generations of women sobbing for the liberty just to undo a button without punishment, choked with the despair of craving to say no, the craving to say I won't, I don't wish to, I'd rather not. She knows because she has overheard them. And she feels her nerveless fingers, dying for the touch of Martin's face, make do with her own, covering her open mouth to stifle the cry that is all ready to break free.

She stares out at the broad oblong of floorboards with its coir runners, its delicate fugitive fluffballs nestling among rigid lines of furniture legs. Blood has soaked into the grain. She knows. Everything repels her and forbids her entry. Here terrors have wept from hurt skin. Here pillows are so stiff with stale tears they need a good pummelling to break up the stuffing and soften them. The kapok mattresses are so packed with fibres glued by salt and menstrual juices they've solidified as lumpy planks beyond bending. The wire bed bases sag under haunches of recollected misery, each one an inheritance of hip-ache and pelvis-barrenness pre-shaped to embrace and cup the next occupant and take her to a familiar place of despair.

The accumulated grief compacts to an invisible wall between Mrs Shoddy and escape.

The juniors glance up at her, as if she has spoken, then silently pursue their duties of cleanliness and order, distributing nighties. Nighties put ready for women desperate to break free into *un*tidiness, women desperate to rediscover some memento of life as it used to be and the living of it, desperate for the *wrongness* of things and for things getting in one's way, for things piled up and hidden, treasures that can be mislaid and tea that can be spilled, desperate for relief from the sheer ache in the heart for lack of someone's eye that can be met, eye to eye, without an assessment being made. Women for whom vomiting vomit is about the only relic of independence they cannot be denied.

The juniors, undaunted, move smoothly and with purpose, rubber-soled shoes suckering across the boards. They are halfway finished and already two of the cupboards with white lattice-wire doors stand empty. They pass in and out of shafts of sunlight. So maybe the only obstacle is Mrs Shoddy's own imagination. Maybe she should chance it, after all. She summons the courage and chooses which way to cross the floor. One of the young women coughs, the delicate feminine sound of a fox, and it's enough to show she's a creature with a pointed nose and possibly claws too, if they could only be seen.

Mrs Shoddy holds back.

The afternoon shadows cast barred netting across the floor right to where her naked feet hesitate at the threshold of the polished surface. She still does not dare place her foot in that net of light, for fear of being snared. Unfed hungers and vile prayers cohere into the substance of the place, its unplumbable reservoir of wretchedness. The uniforms shuttle around more swiftly now. The cough comes again. And Mrs Shoddy recollects sensing someone's presence, many hours previously, right outside her door – *her* door! – while she crouched in the dark, massaging her arms and hands. Mrs Shoddy recollects seeing the peephole cover open to a little disc of yellow electric light. And this is not one of those iris-sized magnifiers private apartments have, but a peephole big as the knob on a cupboard door. Somebody applied their eye on the other side, too, though they couldn't have seen anything because the light was off.

Mrs Shoddy recoils in shock because a figure darts in from the garden and then treads warily her way, watching her.

'Hello, Julie,' Mrs Shoddy says shyly.

'You been asleep a long time.'

'I don't think so.'

'A month seems a long time to us fellows.'

Mrs Shoddy narrows her sore eyes to get the information in focus. A month! Or is this just, she assures herself, a way of talking. An Aboriginal thing.

Next, the woman asks gently, 'Why you here?'

But if ever there was a forbidden subject, this has to be it. She has already been punished for saying she shouldn't be here at all. So, Mrs Shoddy plays for time.

'What's the helmet for?' she asks.

'We got epilepsy. It's to protect us. We got *grand mal* and we fall a lot. Them upstairs don't have to worry. They don't fall much.'

'Do you know Martin?'

'Knew a Martin once. We was kids. He was the Baptist minister's son, way back.'

'I married him.'

'Well, there you go, then, is what I say.'

'What about the telephone? You see, I've got some horses that need water. Can you telephone outside? Someone? If I give you the number?'

'I can't do things for you,' the tea-cosy warns.

Mrs Shoddy decides to retreat from her dangerous hopes. But she needs to keep this contact going.

'He's talking to me, you know,' she says, reverting to the subject of Martin.

'Then let him talk.'

'He loves me.'

'And you're trying to hang on to 'im, ay?'

'But he disappeared.'

love without hope

Julie, who seems to know all about disappearances, simply sucks at her dentures. Her tea-cosy slips a little to one side, but she doesn't bother straightening it. The juniors, indifferent, move in their own space, wordlessly closing wardrobe doors and checking that no pans are left in the night-soil cupboards before one of them slots a key into a little box fitted to the wall, opens it and presses the electric button there, then locks it again.

'What's the button for?' Mrs Shoddy asks.

But Julie starts backing away, eyes filled with fear and shock.

'O my gawd!' she whispers and shields her face.

'What is it?' Mrs Shoddy says, on the verge of stepping out of her cell to comfort the poor creature.

'My gawd!' Julie whispers, backing and retreating, eyes fixed on something just to the side of Mrs Shoddy's door, and makes her wobbly getaway towards the concrete path and the garden.

A bell rings with a stately *dong dang dong*, each sonority echoing for moments afterwards.

Out from behind the door steps the giant, swift and huge in his pale crackling uniform, meaty arms straining the short sleeves, hands thrust forward ready to catch her.

'Not bad,' he admits, 'not at all bad. Sensible choice. If you tried to make a break for it you wouldn't even reach the outer door.'

Mrs Shoddy sees past him, watching the juniors meet each other's eyes as, noiselessly, they close the wardrobes. Julie has gone. Perfect quiet seals the dormitory space. She is trapped again in the Calm Down room, but now she will have new things to remember in the dark when the door is shut. She prays that she will not be strapped to the stretcher, nor forced into a straitjacket again. She prays that Vernon will leave her free to crouch in misery.

'We've had your sort before. With a plan,' he says. 'Do this. Say that. Softly, now. You know?'

Exactly! she thinks as her strength catches up with her palpitations. Amazing, how the weakness took hold of her while she stood on the brink. She learns from it. And Vernon switches on the light so he can eye her with a kind of slumbrous impertinence.

'Is this better?'

It is. Then the latch clicks as he shuts the door after him. She has light.

A letter arrives on Mr Radcliffe's desk, typewritten under an ornate letterhead: *Lunacy Department of New South Wales*. He stands, in order to get at it better, giving himself an advantage. So, ignoring the hospital janitor who sits at the visitors' side of the desk, having just presented an unwelcome report on maintenance problems with the laundry furnace, the Master in Lunacy scans the contents of the letter. Then, exasperated, sits again. He contemplates his faintly trembling hands. This he did not expect. His request to the Minister has been denied. Out of the blue. The janitor, having waited a respectful few minutes, interrupts.

'As I was saying, Mr Radcliffe, I don't see any remedy, other than closing it down and cleaning the whole system.'

Out of the blue.

'The patients can do it,' the Master decides, to shut the fellow up. 'We'll assign a detail to the task.'

But the janitor, in all his odious fleshly solidity, has not done with the role of obstacle.

'I'm afraid this one's beyond them. We're going to need to call someone in from the town.'

To find space and gain time (the really intolerable thing being that the fellow is no doubt right), the Master heaves himself up and crosses to the side window, gazing down at the products of labour below: a tray of bread being carried on someone's head, the sheets on the washing-lines – clean though terminally dingy – snapping their frayed corners, empty wicker baskets set out in regimental order between the poles, the weeded garden beds neat. No escape. He strides back to read that infuriating letter a second time.

Largactil does not have government approval. Though possibly a useful tool in the future for quieting distressed patients, the Department of Health is concerned that this medication may have unforeseen side-effects, therefore... and so forth... and therefore... notwithstanding their recognition of your interest in progress on these fronts and in the light of their high esteem for your record . . . not to mention the taxing work you and your staff undertake . . . inevitably they . . . while wishing you well and . . . so, that's the best we can get from the available . . . sorry . . . very sincerely.

'What action should I take?' the intruder persists.

'I shall look into it,' the Master in Lunacy growls.

With no further comment, the janitor gets up as if to display his compact figure to advantage. Offensively self-effacing and even more offensive in valuing his own competence, he leaves the room.

Martin has been talking again, he's so full of news – such surprising news – incidentally disrupting Lorna's train of thought – which she doesn't want to lose (troubled though it is), because in that swift instant she has caught at the wind-blown hem of a memory: being convinced of the fanciful notion that Nurse Felicity... yes, that Nurse Felicity visited her – even before she knew the nurse's name – because, through some fog of delirium, she recollects the embarrassment of this large female individual handling her bodily in man's hands, stripping her clothes away (yes, surely that did happen) and, when the shameful shit had been sponged off, admitting her damp emaciated tremulous and baby-weak body into the cleft between this same person's breasts – pillowing her there for resuscitation – before treating her like clay, raising her up, moulding and drawing out the new cleanness of her skinny shanks, even to lengthening each finger as one might draw a filament. But Mrs Shoddy does not remember being dressed again, at that time, nor the pain of being strapped back on the pallet.

'Next thing, I found myself arrested,' Martin explains, 'and accused of being an American spy.'

'What!' she says.

'I told them I'm Australian. Same thing, they said. And that's when it hit me. This was serious. And I thought of you, Lorna. It struck me for the very first time how much I've missed you all these years. In that flea-pit of a jail. And I wished I hadn't needed to escape.'

'You could have told me you were leaving.'

'Then it wouldn't have been an escape. And the truth is that I loved being free to come and go as I pleased, I loved having no responsibilities. And I have to confess there were other women. Rather a lot of them. I knew you'd never forgive me if you ever came to know. And that's why I couldn't come home, even when I wanted to. There was no way I could have kept it secret from you. And then it was too late. So I was trapped and, well, put it this way, badly treated. But the point is that I got away. They were moving me from one jail to another when some God-sent terrorist threw a bomb at them. Brilliant.

The long and the short is that I went into hiding. Travelling by foot. You can imagine. Crossing the border under piled-up sacks of rice. Just my kind of thing. And all the while it was you that I kept in mind. The only home I've ever known, really. So, once out of danger I stowed away on a freighter. Ended up in Yokohama, befriended by a family of sisters. Oh well, enough said. And eventually the UK took me in and I began the task of writing it all down. And that was that. The rest of my life lay ahead of me, writing travel books. The attraction of doing something inexcusable, no doubt, instead of just being a cad.'

'But I've been waiting for you.'

'All this time?'

'All this time.'

'You wouldn't approve,' he says after thinking things over. 'I've put on weight.'

She wants to laugh, she wants to cry.

'The good times did the damage. I shaved every single day, can you believe? Very dapper. Louis Feraud made my suits. Some little gnome in Turin fitted me with shoes. God, I had a terrific time. Sorry, old dear, it never crossed my mind that you might agree to come along for the ride, if you were asked. But you wouldn't, would you?'

'I'd like to have been asked.'

But he has gone. Mrs Shoddy has reached a blank. And, next thing, she finds herself out in a different room altogether, flat on her back again and already strapped to that wicker bed she hates so much and, what's more,

love without hope

being set on the carpet in the Master in Lunacy's office with the Master in Lunacy talking down at her. In daylight this room looks bigger, especially from a supine position, the ceiling looks higher, the furniture more massively immovable and the painted-over wallpaper more diseased. Mr Radcliffe, having perched himself on the edge of a studded leather armchair, grows overbearingly confidential. She sees mainly his knees.

'It's a fascinating story we've pieced together. From what you say, your husband survives out there on the fringe as a successful person, the handyman turned travel writer, a racially complex man, can we agree to that, and perhaps culturally confused into the bargain – what with his university studies on top of everything else – still the beneficiary, supposing I may presume some insight, of your infatuation with him. All leading to a glamorous contract with MGM and an all-star cast... may we suppose this the product of many years' risk-taking? Of course, the detail concerns us. So, yes, we are pleased to have it on the record.' (Has she, she wonders uneasily, been talking in her sleep?) 'The operations of the brain and the behaviour of memory – not least the holes and gaps – are understood here, though such matters lie outside my own field of expertise. We have specialists on our staff who assure me they find your case uniquely coherent. Now let me see, what else? The farm, yes. And your bloodstock program for the Australian Walers you breed, the selfsame horses you once exported to fight at Gallipoli, so you say. Or was it *we*, the general public, who exported them? That being seventy years ago, when you were aged . . . three. No wonder you were anxious to share this absorbing stuff and that you felt some urgency about coming to tell me. However, none of this lessens your need of care. Though I should explain that I don't often deal in such matters directly.'

He stands and glows. He turns his back on her. After allowing the silence of power enough time to solidify around them again in this new configuration, his back adds one detail with a summing-up cadence.

'You see, although you have expressed doubts about our methods, we *do* know what we are doing and who we are dealing with. We know what is best for you. The only other possible treatment would be to alleviate your anxiety by administering drugs. Despite the fact that there is one drug which would help, the government, in its wisdom, has not yet released it on to the market. End of story. We can only apologise. Anyway, Lorna,' he faces her again to round it off, bending his eye down on her as she lies at his feet, 'I am very glad to have had the chance of this chat. We are making progress. My task,' he concludes with utterly unfeigned self-compassion, 'is a thankless one. So, every small step forward is an encouragement.'

Scarcely are the words out of his mouth than Mrs Shoddy's world lurches and wobbles as she is picked up by Vernon look-alikes and the corridor gets pulled away like a sleeve from an inert and unwilling arm.

A nice surprise awaits Olga Ostrov, a surprise she thoroughly deserves. True to his promise, Russell Savage has offered her a special deal. Well, he appreciates being able to rely on her. According to him, and speaking as a shire councillor, the essential matter has already been referred to the Public Trustee. The way ahead on that front would appear to be smooth – best to commit as little as necessary to paper, though – but she has his word concerning her own project. And he never reneges on his word. Never. So, when it all goes through, the little block of land she has her eye on will be hers.

Olga, delighted, yields to temptation. Having finished work for the day, she takes a trip over there with the idea of strolling around a bit and sampling a taste of the future.

The last of the light escapes the branches of the two trees the developer has left standing. She can tell, without a doubt, that this is somewhere she will love living. A home she'd hardly dared hope for, the lesson being that nothing can be hurried. Eventualities find their own time and place. She takes a good look at the old milking shed and the houses being built on either side – at various stages of completion and both empty (the workmen having gone home) – then she paces the boundary that is to be hers, spongy tufts of grass giving underfoot. Quite enough for a snug little place, a vege patch and a bit of a native garden. She'll have it looking trim in no time. Soon, in a new development like this, there will be interesting neighbours. People coming down from the city to retire.

It's all she wants: her special patch, with her own view of the mountains.

She has never been greedy. Never. She exhausts herself with good works, helping other people, she surely deserves a little for herself? She just needs to secure a toehold free of entanglements and memories. The stifling grief that has for so long filled her – the buried secret too deep to be dislodged, the fear of burgeoning apple blossoms and roots delving the full length of her legs – begins to shrivel. She will soon open a new chapter.

love without hope

Besides closing the old one. We can't go back, all said and done. Wise to let the past be the past. Put it to rest and get on with life. Loss and anger get no one anywhere. So, things work out for the best, really.

'There's lots to be done,' she says for her own benefit.

She has it all planned. Her little home will boast a courtyard in the Greek style – Olga has travelled, though not (sadly) as far as her grandfather's ancestral home in Sverdlovsk – plus lots of glass facing north because, though she is too well-informed to risk skin cancer by direct exposure to the sun, she needs plenty of light and warmth. She has the style of brick picked out and French windows. She will buy a Westinghouse kitchen and laundry if there's enough cash left over to afford it, so she needn't envy anyone. Till now her life has been hard, with no let-up. She deserves a break. Is she any different from everyone else?

In her heart she finds the reassurance she craves.

No one could wish for such a dull childhood as her parents thrust on her in their frumpy Melbourne suburb: fast food, a black-and-white television in the lounge, herself (at ten) aping the film stars, crimping her hair and having to deal with boys whose sophistication extended so far as to admit there may be other codes of football than Australian Rules, but that no one would be seen dead going to watch them. Her misfortunes included beginning to smoke when she was twelve and never able to give up since. She had had dreadful luck with lovers (or else the worse luck that sex didn't do much for her). Even when she got out and took herself off to Europe at twenty-seven to cope with a suspicion that she might be missing something – as her mother always hinted – Europe proved to be the biggest disappointment. Especially as she kept meeting people along the way who said: Vienna? Why did you choose Vienna? Salzburg's better. Why ever Basel and not Zurich? Copenhagen for goodness' sake! What a shame you missed Berlin. She'd find herself at some famous French cathedral, ticket in hand for the north tower, climbing hundreds of steps, then meeting an enthusiast at the top who explained she'd have been better to climb the south tower if she wanted to see something really exceptional. She'd splurge on a wine from Bordeaux only to find, when she came to recount the story, she'd chosen a château no one ever heard of. She tried escargots in Paris and they gave her food poisoning. She got lost in Hamburg and cried. The wind was against her when she went sailing on the lake at Vinkeveen. In Venice she arrived the very day that rotting little city chose to be half-drowned in knee-high water during *aqua alta* – wouldn't you know? – and rendered the whole place insufferable. Even her bus tour of Rome was ruined by a gossipy American sitting next to her, for whom no sight was sufficient without being named and exclaimed upon. She did reach Russia, in the end, just the tip of it. But instead of loving the land of her ancestors she simply froze. Famously warm and warm-blooded as she was, it took Russia to teach her about the cold. What's worse, some pickpocket filched her purse in St Petersburg (of all places)

love without hope

and people merely stared when she started screaming *But I'm one of you!*

Not to be thought about. She has sworn to put it behind her. She laughs at the idea of travel enriching the mind. She considers ethnic food, of whatever type, best cooked in Australia. She no longer even speaks to her mother. She has a good job, helping people who cannot help themselves and (as she herself repeatedly says) she has become an identity around this little town since settling here. So, put that in your pipe.

She has stuck it out, her life, toiler that she is. Olga Ostrov's a battler and one of the people, after all. She takes a last longing look around the block of land and then checks her diary. She's due to call on Elsie Southwell.

Dr Parker crams his hat on his head and storms out, stick in hand, along the main street. His fury like a pack of dogs crowding around him, now and again tripping him in their eagerness, brushing his trouser legs with their indigo fur and turning to check his bloodshot eyes with theirs. The Noone brat, Brad, seeing him go by, throws a stone at him intending to miss but very nearly hitting him because, at this moment, the old man baulks before some invisible obstacle, some upstart pothole or gaping pit of serpents, which he must step over or stamp underfoot. And, resuming his trajectory

love without hope

(as one who attains the crest and can now plunge downhill), he rushes to the crux of the conflict, winged along by the flutterings of his coat tatters, his teeth meanwhile grinding audible syllables to be spat out as bitter gobs of pulp.

'How dare he! He knows the etiquette. Nothing's ever been heard to equal it.'

Dr Parker, who advocates the old values, a tradition of professional courtesy, has so far borne the insult of a second practice being set up in town without his agreement. Hasn't he grimly refused to comment, even to his friends, on the young doctor's presumption? But this latest outrage is the scandalous limit. He stamps and tromps and blunders down past the pub, past the bakery, nodding at Mike Noone the butcher, father of the brat (who *was* seen throwing his stone) as he adds a tray of liver to the lurid raw flesh display in his window. Dr Parker boils on past the snack bar, where the odious Savage creature transacts shady deals in property, a creep if ever there was one! His wrath barges ahead, grabbing for the door to that surgery he has never set foot in till now, nor wished to. He clutches, seizes, he wrenches, he flings the door wide. The opening of the door alone burns away the last vestiges of the previous night's gin and his mind is clear.

An O'Hare girl glances up from behind the enquiry desk, a startled look in which some shrinking admission slides off to one corner of her eye. Before she can unglue her Revlon lips to give utterance to the protest she knows must be made, he has reached the inner room, which he opens to reveal an astonished publican in the act of laying bare the sunless skin of his ulcerated leg and stopping mid-sentence in his complaint against the pain.

'Get out of my way,' Dr Parker roars at him, slashing the air with his walking stick. 'I told you to see me about that leg months ago.'

The young doctor has already sprung to his feet with the elasticity of a basketball player, the dangerous blood of a long-postponed joy surging through him.

'That bitch of a public nurse,' Dr Parker hurls at him, 'she knows. She knows. She had no right to refer the case to you.' His body piles up its steaming masses of indignation. 'Mrs Shoddy is my patient. My patient. Indisputably mine and has been since before you were born. Did she ever consult you? Ever? No! And you know it. You've nothing to say for yourself because you cannot avoid the truth of what I say. Well might you stand there like ... like ... like the gormless spineless conniving cold-hearted cynic you've proved yourself to be by signing that document. What harm?' he shouts hoarsely. 'What harm has she done anyone? Least of all you? By what possible perversion of reason could a woman like that be committed? A woman who fends for herself and raises horses? A woman who has lived there most of her life? No decent human being could help feeling, let me assure you, in any reasoned calm sober evaluation, inexpressible contempt for what you are, you soiled puppy, and for what you've done.'

love without hope

The publican, who is rumoured to have grown rich on gin sales, covers his disgusting leg and stands lopsidedly. Meanwhile the young doctor, having collected himself, adds the telephone to the armoury of a powerful fist.

'Call the policeman, Miss O'Hare.'

'*He's* in it too,' Dr Parker thunders contemptuously. 'He has to be.'

'Tell him to hurry before I lose my temper. Tell him to come now. Or he'll have to carry this drunk out of my surgery.'

M rs Shoddy is writing a letter in her head. This letter has been many times written. Now, at last, in her head, she sends it:

> *What I have not been able to say to you is that I knew you would have to leave one day. What I have not been able to say to you is that I was going to suggest it anyway. You need your freedom. And one thing I always understood was that we never meant the same thing by Home.*
>
> *But that was in the days when I thought I could do without you.*

love without hope

Even so, I do wish I had made the offer because it might have made a difference.

So, maybe all I need say is that when you come back you will find me waiting. And I won't ask a single thing. What has passed has passed. Let there be silence between us, a silence in which I can lose even the words of the wishes I'm wishing right now while I struggle to summon you here.

You'll find me in an asylum for the insane and you'll have to get me out. As a spy you must have all sorts of skills. And you are clever enough for anything. The head man, Mr Bevis Radcliffe, can, I think, be talked to. But don't have anything to do with a nurse called Vernon. Vernon is my enemy. He will tell you I am mad. Do not believe him. Kill him before you believe him. I am the same old Lorna, though I'm afraid you'll find me a shadow of the woman I was.

As for your ambition to escape so you can take fresh risks, the next one I am asking you to consider is to start a new life with me. Martin, wanting you as I do, I don't care what you've done or where you've been. Believe me, I shall not pry into your secrets. I shall embrace you. And then I shall sleep.

Mrs Shoddy has not slept. She crouches in a frog-slime of creeping light. And now the door opens on the dormitory darkness to let in a tide of smothered pandemonium. And while she listens to the panic of those who cannot endure their lonely dreams a torch casts its wavering beam to wake shadows and set them swooping hugely, shadows that dwindle, squat as dwarves in the corners, or glide up across the ceiling and down the other side to stand against the wall like a second inspectorial person.

The figure holding the torch fills the doorway.

'Why are you here?' Mrs Shoddy asks.

And goosebumps set her skin shuddering.

'I brought another blanket,' says a voice she knows.

The shadow comes in and pulls the door closed, then displays colossal wings to show her.

'I'm afraid,' Mrs Shoddy whispers in the sleepless nightmare of her life.

'Shall I hold your hand a while?'

'No.'

Next thing, the blanket swoops on Mrs Shoddy to smother her. She wriggles under bulky folds, she fights the disinfected density, overcome as catatonia seizes her limbs and pins her to the floor, paralysed under a covering thick as turf, a burial mound so slightly heaped up over her it is scarcely more than flat, and herself so close to death she scarcely breathes in there.

'Calm now,' Nurse Felicity murmurs, 'calm now.'

And she seeks Mrs Shoddy's hand beneath the folds, discovering it and taking that cold little bunch of appendages into her own warm keeping.

'Calm now,' Felicity murmurs again. 'It's nothing but the dark.'

Dr Parker has also written a letter, but in his case he has the envelope ready and complete with stamp. Fountain pen in hand he answers a telephone call. This is the call he has been expecting. In the dashing manner of written prescriptions he scrawls the Queensland address he is given. And draws an emphatic line under it.

'Thank you,' he says. Remembering to add as he hangs up, 'Good work.'

He licks the flap and seals the envelope. Shaky though he feels, there is not a moment to lose. He takes his stick and sets off for the post office immediately.

Vernon Ross has a special interest in divinity and spends much of his spare time delving into the labyrinth of cosmology. Well, he needs relief from duty and the conversation of lunatics. There are times, as he tells himself, when survival itself depends upon asserting one's right to a life of one's own. And a frank acknowledgement of intellectual superiority. Exactly. Why else does he entertain himself with TV quiz shows? Why else has he become a regular at the Public Library, hunched over his little hardback notebook, transcribing what he needs to remember? Why else has he developed the habit, back in the privacy of his room, of talking to himself (that old chestnut about the first sign of madness being nonsense and mere superstition), discussing the day's new ideas? Because he does talk. Out loud. Which reassures him. As – right now – he throws himself on to the couch to review the latest developments of his special subject. 'That's it. Because I . . . we, if we're halfway alive, need . . . don't we all? *The idea of divinity, as symbolic, represents the human struggle* exactly, exactly *at its highest: mankind's effort to discover our identity* yes and this puts it really well *as we confront the limits of our universe*. We do have to care about the – seek the – big picture.' He licks his finger and flips a page. '*In his journey toward self-identity man encounters divinity.* Very true. Ah, how I feel a . . . love this, this, love exercising the mind, the muscle of the mind. That's it.' Basking. 'What's the answer for a thousand dollars? What does the idea of divinity represent?' 'Um – the human struggle at its highest.' 'Yes! You have won. That was a great round, Vernon. I am pleased to say this earns you a crack at our jackpot. How do you feel?' 'Um – like basking in the, under a ray-lamp, really.' 'Ha ha. It takes all types.' And he does feel his relaxing flesh expand. The couch supports him. 'What? What else?' *The very idea of divinity liberates us from the weight of selfishness, permitting us to soar.* 'Well, that's my strength.' I wouldn't think anybody could call me selfish: not a single soul out there, or in the wards. Strict, in my way. 'Yes, because.' And reliable, certainly. 'But still fair. You know?' That's right: we are liberated by . . . liberty. Is liberty what . . .? 'Never mind.' Plus, on a daily basis. If only. Is it asking too much for others to th–, for me to be thanked? 'Evidently is.' And, when you come to think, who else is there? 'Nobody.' Just me. In this place. And that's not vanity, that's the truth, the truth, inescapably. 'The inescapable truth.' What else? *As such, the notion of divinity becomes symbolic of human perfection, an escape from man's often painful limitations.* To what we're meant to be. If there is a 'meant'. *It has its origin in the existential anxiety of the human-being faced with the mysteries of life and nature. Hence, the appeal of the fully divinized man: Christ.*

Vernon reaches for his glass of beer. His gaze chances out through the window where a stone cross surmounts the gabled roof of the Court of Lunacy. Well, there's no such thing as coincidence, really. A timely reminder.

'So is that how we could, how we do describe Jesus? Human perfection.' And us needing him because we're in, what was it, existential anxiety, faced with the mysteries of life? *Sceptics would say the idea of divinity is a mere illusion perpetrated to console us in our impotence.* 'No doubt.' Sceptics and betrayers both.

He sucks on the beer, nodding at his own grasp and wisdom, wondering about betrayers, about Judas, wondering about Pontius Pilate. He once read that scholars believe Pontius Pilate might have been a Scot, born in the old royal capital Scone, Perthshire (as was his own father), which interests him more than the rival claim

love without hope

that the great man might, alternatively, have been German (such was the Roman Empire with its polar policy of promotions in foreign territory, its African legions in Gaul, its Romanians in Algiers). 'But was he, strictly, a betrayer like Judas?' Pilate can be imagined, with his dignified bearing and his toga. But Judas? Did Judas's everyday behaviour offer a clue? Apparently not, or no one would have trusted him in the first place. 'A betrayer must be trusted.' And how would Judas walk the world out there if he came back? Let loose in an international crisis between Communism and us? Like James Bond. Maybe, because there must *be* Judases among us. 'But how did he die?' Does the Bible tell us? It's a tough one. A real question.

'Now for the final test. Who was the, watch out for this, Vernon, this is a trick question, who was the most beloved disciple? It's a deep one. What's your answer? You have another five seconds, Vernon.' 'Okay, I'm ready. I'm going for Judas.' 'Judas is . . . right! You've just earned yourself a place in our Hall of Fame. What made you pick Judas and not Peter or John?' 'I just . . . well, I thought it out. I've given it a lot of thought over the . . .' 'You're a thinking man, aren't you?' '. . . over the years.' 'Is that what you'd call yourself, a thinking man?' 'Yes, I would.' 'Fair enough and I believe our studio audience might agree. What do you say, folks? So, why Judas as the most beloved?' 'Well, because he was the most important. I mean, even Peter got no further than three times denying. Judas actually went the whole hog (if I'm allowed to speak bluntly on TV) and saw to it that Jesus was crucified. Without the crucifixion there would have been no rising from the dead three days later, no church, no Christianity, really.' 'Very good, you're very good.'

Vernon drains his glass and hoists himself to his feet. 'Oh, bullshit. Why do I waste my time?' He strolls into the bathroom. 'But still,' he objects against his own objection, 'there's something in it. We don't, we can't, say much about Judas. Just that he – kind of – came out of nowhere. The unpredictable. A man who escaped notice.' He unzips his pants and takes a piss, remembering to spare his penis a brief admiring glance. 'Nothing gave *him* away. He was too ordinary. Yet somehow he found the courage. And BAM! the king hit. Up till then he was just one of the crowd.' He shakes off some drops and bares his teeth at the mirror. Time for the gym.

J ust exactly when the rain began, Mrs Shoddy has no way of knowing, but once she wakes up to it she finds a lot of other things have changed as well. For a start, she has been allocated a place in the dormitory. And here she is, standing on her own two feet beside a blessed creaky bed, shivering her way into the miserable clothes they issue her with. Her arms are not strapped to her sides. So now, she is like everybody else, at last: an ageless automaton whose oppression can be regarded as routine. She has forgotten who she used to be, let alone why she agreed to come. Enough that she accepts the sounding of the bell, the folding of nighties, the spooning of breakfast porridge into her mouth, the lining up for hot cocoa and, when it comes to the point, the sudden realisation that what she thought was the roar of a decayed building in collapse around her – her own inexorable slow-motion burial under rubble – is not the building at all.

The others crowd the doorways and she joins them to watch plummeting iron raindrops shoot at the earth with the force of bullets. A foamy surplus from the gutter already froths over the lip and dribbles from crossbeams and window sashes. The smell of blood in the air is sucked from the dormitory, together with such warmth as eighty bodies accumulate by slow respiration throughout the night, and stretched like skin, glazed skin, out over the concrete paths to mirror the fat splashy myriad drops.

'It's because he's goin' to die,' Julie explains, 'all this.' And she indicates the rain.

'Who?'

'Old Tom, I reckon.'

Tom Hopkinson, the longest surviving among them all. Mrs Shoddy doesn't know him – how could she? – yet she feels his impending loss. She looks and she thinks. Sad ropes of transparent water-muscles uncoil the length of the street right down to where they spool into the sinkhole, their sheer volume baffling grids and gratings. Tree branches bend and fracture under the weight of the deluge. Rain, as a million-spiked rasp, scours all colour and substance from the buildings across the yard (includ-

love without hope

ing the administration block, the so-called Court of Lunacy), while slate roofs are angle-ground to the sharpness of knives. She marvels at the storm from where she stands among less fortunate women who prop their wreckage on walking frames, or waver fearfully, paralysed by doubt, up against the insuperable obstacle of a decision: to stay or go back indoors.

Mrs Shoddy marvels at the beauty of surplus run-off whirlpooling into an open trench exactly the way it did when she was a child. Rainwater sloshes over fire bucket rims and ripples down walls under blackly-jutting gables that strike her as desperate vessels in a choppy sea – ships foundering amid spray thick as smoke – and even the hospital clock-tower survives only as a despairing remnant of the same wreckage, while its bell, jostled into motion by no human hand, faintly plaintively tolls.

An anarchy of persistence, the rain rains and rains, reinventing water, sweeping swarms of grasshoppers from the sky, knocking birds askew mid-flight, rolling a dead dog in through the gate, flooding and choking, choking and flooding the roadway outside, swirling down the hill, swish-swirling to inundate the tidy flowerbeds of the sane (across the road), the meticulous obsessions of the not-mad in their suburban alienation, flushing clumps of irises out of the soil and already tumbling their mat of tangled bulbs and roots in a hectic caracole over the pedestrian crossing out beyond the garden wall.

She watches, enchanted.

This rain has become the rule of the absolute, a torment, a tyrant, a rebuke, welling to submerge the rim of ponds and pools while the creek itself, down there under its appointed bridge, begins to climb free... creeping up the bank toward the feet of some concerned citizens (just visible to Mrs Shoddy through a screen of trees), gathering to keep watch over it. Telegraph wires drip on a sodden fugitive postman doomed to ply his obligations. Cattle in the slaughter yards bellow bewilderedly while a creeping damp, as capacious as Australia, rises through earth's crust to mulch it with mucilaginous and treacherous side-slipping logic, the overthrow of the laws of gravitation, everything deteriorating in slanted planes and nothing left firmly perpendicular – the rain itself leans, as she plainly sees, a bend in the gravitational pull, a world-warping swerve.

Even during that moment, as Mrs Shoddy stands in the doorway feeling the heavy ball of porridge lower itself cautiously into her stomach, she finds she can breathe the rain. Such joy! Swamped with memories and grief, she reaches out her frail hands to feel nails pass through them. She knows her beloved horses are dead, dead as that stiff-legged swollen dog, dead in their sleep one night (having packed up their contented memories of her care), cushion tongues protruding uselessly, their long hollow-structured cheeks and tender nostrils, their great luminous eyes turned to the sky and washed out.

She advances her own nose on a cluster of climbing roses and this reminds her.

love without hope

The other inmates grow bored and wander back inside to resume rostered tasks of bread-making, toilet-sluicing and canvas-stitching. Only the ladies slated for garden duties linger in a cluster under a covered walkway in the slice of dryness sandwiched between parallel curtains of rain, sharing their bafflement with a matching cluster of men on the other side of the quadrangle, one of whom, a shocked looking scarecrow even older than Mrs Shoddy herself, hunkers down, clutching at his heart, a mere dandelion-head of a man who, at a touch, would surely break apart into scatterings of *she loves me*s and *she loves me not*s. Whatever flesh tint may once have coloured his skin has long since desiccated and drifted away as dandruff on the wind. He remains as the last relic and shrivelled heart of dryness.

Mrs Shoddy takes note of him. Then proceeds to look the other men over. Such is her interest that all males get taken account of and subjected to her telescoping intense impotent scrutiny ... well, in case he might betray some sign of being Martin – Martin, back from Hvar and free of that bigamous wife (who is welcome to keep her diamonds, so long as she surrenders him). No luck. And certainly none where these garden troglodytes are concerned. Nevertheless, she is curious to see if any of them will dare trespass into the downpour. And somehow this sets a peculiar feeling going, a feeling without name or direction, simply some disturbance of her hibernation. Alert, she asks the feeling what it is. She asks it for a word, a single word, by which she might know it. Blood racing in anticipation, she asks the din of the deluge – but the only word she is to be given is offered by one of the junior nurses, who tugs her sleeve and steers her back inside.

'Lorna, Lorna,' the nurse says, '*Lorna!*'

So she comes to unstick herself from the fascination, the mesmerising swerve of sky. Even to hearing herself being told to help carry some night-soil buckets out.

'Where's Felicity?' Mrs Shoddy asks irritably.

'She's never on duty in the morning. She has to sleep sometime.'

To Mrs Shoddy the dormitory looks somehow unfamiliar. The cupboards stand open. The wardrobes stand open. The barred doors to the confinement cells stand open. Even the door with its peephole, the most dreaded door to the Calm Down room, that old dungeon she used to be in, stands open. And the entire space of comfortless echoes is sighing at the pitch of the torn rain. While she, hollow-mouthed like the cupboards, witnesses a tragedy happening right before her eyes. Yes, the place is a stage... as she had immediately seen that time when she got her first good look and Julie – once again centre-stage, as she had been before – hovers alone in the spotlight. Julie's rope-helmeted head shows itself at the wrong angle, twisting her neck so that it must surely unbalance her altogether. The head, appearing to drag the body beneath, yanks her up off the floor, then hurls her to one side, floppy limbs whipping about, fingers snapping at nothing. Now the helmet charges at a pillar in the middle of the floor, so dreadfully butting against it her shoulders are jolted out of joint and each impact shudders down through those comfortable cushions of her body till the bones fold, compacted. Only to rebound, catapulting her rigid. She is a diver, diving for the ceiling, levitating at a slant (and impossibly suspended for a long-drawn moment), before the mechanism retracts to hurl her, all balled up, at the cold pot-bellied stove. More: the helmet, not yet satisfied, jerks her along the coir mat, flipping her bodily to make sure her face is scoured by it, trundling her on her side like a piece of meat, raising one leg to point the toe in a gesture from the ballet, meanwhile her scream – uttered minutes earlier – finally reaches the ear and reaches the recoiling brain, its operatic note lustrous with hair-raising power, a scream she then sucks back into her mouth and swallows, only to feed it out again as froth.

Mrs Shoddy's body is locked where Mrs Shoddy's spirit left it. Mrs Shoddy's spirit is by Julie's side, caressing her and murmuring soothing reassurances, Mrs Shoddy's spirit is in grief and terror while covering her friend's shame from that boggling mob of fellow creatures, all but a few of whom wear similar padded headpieces ready for their own star turn. And from the elbowing junior staff who take a good look at what they must learn to treat as mundane, while the Day Sister kneels to get better purchase as she thrusts a wad of cotton between Julie's teeth and wrestles against the dancing angel.

Mrs Shoddy trusts her spirit to help comfort Julie. But, in a flash of intuition, she knows this crisis is being played out for her sake. She knows this is meant for her, this savage banal transfiguration is a gift she cannot refuse. Julie, as the one who offers the gift, must not come round to find she has suffered for nothing and that Mrs Shoddy is still here. The sacrifice wasted.

So, Mrs Shoddy shuts her eyes against being noticed and allows hearing to guide her. She is drawn again to the storm, its thunder of a doomed building stupendous enough to muffle the knocking of her heart. Julie sustains the frothing and tremors to make this possible, her crooked rope helmet thudding at the boards, each muted impact in the rhythm of reiterations: *go, go, go now, go now, go now*. And, obediently, Mrs Shoddy finds she can shuffle like a blind shadow, away, backing off, creeping aside, sidling to the door, down the open passage, drawn toward the embrace of that thunderous downpour. No longer aware of her pulsing fear, she thrills to a flutter of excitement. She reaches the porch and no one is there to stop her or send her back.

She opens her eyes on the sudden aluminium-bright torrent of rain. Promptly stepping into the cold shock of it, needled, confronted by a maze of bead-curtains, she feels herself rise inside a rainbow, hope swelling her pitiful chest as she clutches her scalp, exposed now to the sheer light arcing radiantly up into the tumbling sky. Hair plastered like paint, her flesh didders and her shadow streams down into its own reflection, as she ghosts right into the cascading heart of the music engulfing her in harmony. A cataract of semi-quavers shimmers and dances, atomising her silhouette at the blurred boundaries of a vast anthem, then bundles her across the yard, across the encircling lawn, past the hospital cricket ground with its grandstand, out through the tradesmen's gate and down the lane towards a torrent of waters intermingling to engulf the bridge – gushing bright with coloured rubbish and broken saplings – where even the frogs sound like little musical pots.

A bridge.

Here she can cross over to the other side. And she does, joining the watchers gathered there and standing among them, as if she is one of the fortunate, even looking back at the way she has come, into the prayer she once prayed: *Thou hast been our dwelling place. O God our help in ages past*, seeing, through spangled eyelashes, the hospital buildings (complete with belltower) erased, entirely dissolved and overwhelmed: *Our hope for years to come*. Unaware of the neighbourly person sharing an umbrella to shelter her, she is also oblivious to her own stuck and sodden smock, a garment stripped of any uniform-stigma (or even shape) by its new status as wet rag. Her shivering turns into giggles. Like a girl, she laughs up at the smiling face of the umbrella lady. And this person likes her, though they haven't met. There is no separating joy from grief, ecstasy from debasement, it is all one harmony, one concord of belonging. Just so, she is free to leave, even as she came. She turns her back on the people she has anonymously joined. She steps it out again, in tempo with the solemn joyful serenity of confusion: *Our shelter from the stormy blast. We spend our years as a tale that is told.* She dwindles, blurred and shrouded, a tiny corrosion of the immensity around her.

The storm exists as pure sound. Rain coheres to a quality of stillness, filling all space, binding sky to earth as a seamless stationary tapestry of diamonds, and Mrs Shoddy – going she knows not where – moves in jerky diminutions, suspended from snapping threads, like a puppet in the wavering eyes of a sleepy child, tinier and frailer, hesitantly farther off, drawn away and away, till she entirely disappears in the music.

Arthur Gibbons, Rita's husband, ventures to ask her who keeps leaving telephone messages about some parcel of land or other? Well, because, as he explains (his tone already foreshadowing a retreat in case she contests his right and brings out the heavy artillery of her outraged family), this is the third time. She stands stonily at the sink – interrupted in the midst of clarifying her strategy for bringing the Sewing Circle to heel over the matter of a collective quilt and whose portrait it should represent – because she still hasn't decided how to handle her spot of good luck, as it might be called.

'I'm sick of nosy parkers,' she states, flicking suds from her fingers and throwing words for him, much as she might throw scraps for a dog to catch in its teeth.

Arthur Gibbons has his share of cunning and, of course, he knows she is devoted to him.

'So, shall *I* ring this one for you, love?'

'You!'

He recoils from the sharpness of her reaction.

'He left a number.'

'I dare say he did. These callers are forever leaving numbers, leaving them here, leaving them at the CWA, leaving them just about anywhere. And talking to just about anybody. I don't mind saying I regret ever having the least thing to do with this business.'

'So, you *did!*'

'Did what?' her walking headache demands.

'Have something to do with something.'

'I did nothing. Nothing but a community service. A kindness. I should have known better. I gather this all has some connection with Lorna Shoddy. But if it's to do with her being taken to hospital they should speak to Olga about the state she was in. Though I'm sure I don't know why my number was ever given out. I mean – why mine? Olga's got the phone on down at the caravan park. Or, at least, they have one in the office there. I do hate a mystery.'

'Me too, love,' he contributes slyly. 'What age would this man be?'

love without hope

'How am I to know a thing like that? How in the name of all that's wonderful?'

Mr Gibbons, one time shire clerk and a citizen who still values a peaceful beer and a yarn with the boys, backs off by tucking his chin in. And she sees it.

'What was the latest, anyway?' she retracts so far as to demand.

Her husband settles permanently in his chair, opens the newspaper and peeps over the battlements before responding.

'A message to make sure Russell Savage *gets the nod*, so he said.'

'Well, I'm sure I can't imagine what that's supposed to mean.'

'I wrote it down here,' and he passes her the note.

Says he needs a decision. Any complications – the deal is off.

Rita stares at it, then returns her attention to sluicing the lunch dishes. She suspects something. She should investigate. Keep her eyes open. Especially in a small town like this. And being a person born into a pioneer family. She comes to a decision.

'This is all double-Dutch to me. Nevertheless, I suppose I shall have to take my umbrella and go down there. I shall give her a piece of my mind, I can assure you.'

'Why don't you ring the office, like you said *he* should.'

That does it.

'Because I mind my own business,' she snaps at her old darling.

Rita Gibbons has more to put up with than most. And now this phone message nuisance. She balances her aching head. She wipes her hands on a teatowel. There's definitely something fishy. People can say what they like about Olga, Olga comes from the city and she's a different sort of person who doesn't know how things should be done. Not like a countrywoman. Already out and on her way, despite a brewing storm, and opening her umbrella against a tentative scatter of rain, Rita Gibbons gets a good look at the colossal blue-black ochre-bellied cloud extending inland the full length of the horizon.

'There'll be floods somewhere,' she greets her neighbour opposite (a Queenslander) with grim satisfaction.

She's off, portly and unstoppable, rickety as ever, her umbrella a declaration, crowded as it is with big red poppies, ambling past the shire office and the library, past the vet, past the hardware store and in at the driveway to the caravan park. She nods to commiserate with a tourist hastily stripping her washing from the rotary hoist, but withholds any chitchat because you never know who it might be. Better not raise too many hopes in an unknown visitor. Then she's opening the screen door, cooeeing at the caravan window. Eventually an irate face presents itself on the other side of the flywire.

'What is it?' Olga snaps.

'Olga?'

love without hope

'Rita! Can I . . .?'

'I got a phone message. Something about Russell Savage. And all because of you. Open up. Now look, Olga, this has to stop. My Arthur is most disapproving. He's very jealous, you know. I mean to say: calls from a stranger – and a man. Ringin' me at the CWA, which the whole world and its dog knows about. Then ringin' me at home when I'm not there.'

The flimsy squeaking door is unclipped from the inside.

'I hear what you're saying, Rita. Do come in, you'll get soaked. But – yes, come in – it's because you're the one person in town whose opinion can be depended on. In such confidential circumstances.'

The caravan sways as Mrs Gibbons steps up. In the kitchenette she squeezes herself into a little fixed bench on one side of the little fixed table, while her hostess slips into the other, and so the battle lines are drawn, if it's to be a battle. They share a pot of tea and munch on Nice biscuits. Olga dusts her fingers politely.

'As I've already said to you, I believe there might be a small, I'm afraid, very small commission in this. For someone willing to pass messages. I can't be more specific than that, really. Something more like a *reward*,' she corrects herself. 'Because negotiations have to remain nameless just at present. And I've no doubt whoever comes up with the best offer will agree that a modest thank you would be only fair. Mind, I can't promise. I can't speak on anyone's behalf. And I have to keep right out of it. My professional good name is at stake. The best I can do is hint. And I will. I promise you that.'

Rita Gibbons's silence is provisional. The walk has cleared her headache so the formidable mechanisms of her brain get busy unencumbered. She reviews the advantages. She does have the nest-egg her mother left her all those years ago, of course, but the thought of adding to it – even a little – would mean she could take some pride in revisiting her will. There being some recent scores to settle. And the young ones need to be brought to heel.

'I mean, just privately,' the district nurse confides. 'Between ourselves. The less said the better.'

Mrs Gibbons considers her tired old diamond and her wedding band, then turns her hands over – well, because they look better that way, the palms being less wrinkled – and she sighs. Who can say she has done anything wrong if she hasn't the foggiest what this is all leading to? She weighs balls of nothingness in her cupped hands.

'I don't want you to feel in any way compromised, Rita,' Olga takes it up again, her manner neither warm nor cold. 'Not at all. But, I believe a lot of money is at stake. Though of course there's absolutely nothing in it for me. No doubt Russell has his reasons for wanting to keep everything confidential. He is a councillor, after all, and the council is foreclosing on account of rates in arrears.'

Mrs Gibbons has been digesting her biscuit. She aims a late shot.

love without hope

'Though why mention the CWA?'

'That's obvious. Everyone knows and respects the CWA. And you, being president ... represent what's trustworthy. A pillar of the community. But since it's Lorna Shoddy's old place, I mean to say, *I* couldn't be caught mentioning a single word about any such thing. If anyone overheard! Phone taps. Whatever. I have my job to think of. And my patients. I must stay completely in the clear because someone has to help, now that the poor woman can no longer help herself.'

'Well,' Rita has reached her verdict. She drains the cup and announces sternly, 'I should hope you really *are* in the clear.'

'I'd never take advantage of anyone. It makes me shudder to think of.'

'Nothing would induce *me* to poke my nose in where it isn't wanted. Though a gesture of thanks is another matter. The poor thing. It's a courtesy, wouldn't you say?'

'Exactly.'

Olga doesn't venture any further speculation.

So, Rita Gibbons, having said what she came to say, extricates herself from the table legs and lumbers out through the screen door. Setting off home. Her dome of poppies abruptly flowering against the drizzle, vivid as splashes of blood. Olga watches her go. The rumble of thunder rolls closer. And a more serious commitment by the rain sets in.

Russell Savage, pacing the confines of his snack bar-cum-real estate agency, refuses to meet his wife's eye. Indeed, he considers the advantages of murdering her. The more he thinks about it, the worse his mistake: marrying her in the first place. But divorce is out of the question, the courts would strip him of his assets. Meanwhile, she's driving him crazy with her senseless prattle. The stuff this stupid bitch picks up from women's magazines, the endless sewer of gossip about film stars and – for the love of Christ – the sodding Royal Family! He's trapped. Desperate. Longing for those few brief

love without hope

years when he was single and an accountant. And now she behaves (he explains to himself) as if she's on to something. She nags and nags. That *voice!* Just the sound of it! So, where does she get the sudden idea she can question him? Right now she's giving him a look as if he has been caught backing off. He never backed off in his life.

'So?' Gail persists meekly.

He's not used to this. He doesn't like it. He won't put up with any more. Her drivel's going to drive him nuts. Not to mention her presumption. All brought on by what? Nothing. Olga Ostrov was seen coming out of his office again. So? Is that the sum total of his crime? For God's sake! Anyone would think he was having an affair with the woman! Questions, questions. Seriously, any more of this and the whole plan could be at risk.

'So, why was she here?' Gail persists.

'What makes you think she wasn't just buying a sandwich?' he shouts.

'You're shouting, that's what.'

'She's on at me about that Woodland Estate place she wants.'

'She looked happy.'

'She might have scrounged the money for it, who knows?'

'I saw her prancing.'

'The bank might have lent it to her.'

'That's not what you said yesterday.'

'Yesterday I wasn't driven out of my mind by your interruptions.'

Nevertheless, Gail's hair sparks with defiance as she sticks to her point.

'So why did she pretend not to see me?'

'Maybe because she didn't see you?'

'She looked furtive. Happy and furtive.'

'Where would you find words like *furtive* and *prancing*?'

'I know. I know there's something going on. And I have a right.'

'You have bugger-all right,' he seethes. 'Keep out of it.'

'So, there is something to be kept out of!'

He has put up with more than enough. What's chaining him to the fucking woman, when it comes to the crunch? What's chaining him to this fucking town, for that matter? Well, give or take a week or two, he'll be able to afford to make a move. Clear out. Shake off his worries. If only he could shake Gail off with them. Soon enough he'll be too old to cut loose, after all. Proof being his beer gut. Life is escaping him.

Stamping up and down behind the counter, distractedly noticing the passing traffic, Russell Savage considers the advantages of murdering his wife.

The Master in Lunacy's title has been taken from him. According to the Department (having surrendered its own ancient dignity as the Department of Lunacy, to be subsumed into the greater good of the Department of Health), he is now to be addressed as Superintendent. The shingle has already been removed from his door, awaiting replacement. He mightn't like the change, but the government gives him no choice. His building, the Court of Lunacy, is to be called the Administration Office. There are other changes, too, even affecting standards of treatment. Who knows? Next thing, the leather handcuffs and bed straps, still in use, might soon have to be abandoned. Even the Calm Down rooms may be closed for good. These decisions – made by politicians with no practical experience of the patients' needs, let alone the consequences of such measures – are plainly ideological. Naturally, he voiced his unease. But no one paid the least attention. Now all he can do is accept the bitter fact.

Coincidentally, the laundry furnace has broken down, exactly as the janitor predicted. The maddening thing is that nobody can be blamed, an overhaul was slated for this very morning. But who could have foreseen the eventuality of a colossal storm bringing the town to a standstill? Which is exactly what happens. He stares, for proof, at the curtains of rain out there. His view of the town wiped out. Wind whipping up such chaos branches are ripped off trees to fall across the way. The traffic stops. Gusts dash themselves against his windows till he can barely see past the front gate to the houses across the street. Eyes blank with frustration, he gazes at the weather, sunk in melancholy, numb to the existence of his own body, incapable of movement. The sky expunged. The glass pitted. The entire population might as well have died. Nothing left but the deluge. That and, surprisingly, vehicle headlamps. A vehicle approaching down the hill. Such a day to be on the street! Could this be the mechanic, after all? Yellow beams cut horizontal slices through the white-out of rain. And yes – how amazing – the headlights turn in at the hospital entry.

love without hope

But, no. He sees now that the car drawing to a halt in the driveway below him is a BMW. So, this can't be the mechanic. Well, the staff will deal with it.

And that's just what happens because, five minutes later, his secretary ventures in to deliver a visiting card, a card evidently printed long ago, an engraved card (that anachronistic dignity) bearing no address, no telephone number, no profession. Commandingly austere, it reads: *Archibald Parker B.Sc., M.D.* Odd. Mr Radcliffe, priding himself on some acumen as a detective, sets his deductive skills to work. Who? An older man, evidently. A man who values reticence. A confident man. Doubtless a medical practitioner interested in the care of the insane. The Superintendent has it all down pat. Well, of course, he will see his visitor. On such a day. With pleasure. And Dr Parker, when shown in, exactly answers expectations. Most satisfactory. His baggy old suit well-cut, his bow tie carelessly elegant, his dipsomaniac's nose large, his slouch encumbered, his shoes good quality, his walking stick silver-capped and his manner courtly. He makes a substantial, not to say ponderous, impression.

'I am here,' the stranger announces without preamble, 'to see my patient, Mrs Lorna Shoddy.'

'Lorna?'

'Mrs Shoddy.'

'Were we expecting you?'

'I set out at short notice.'

'You have come a long way?'

'Too long.'

'May I offer you a cup of tea?'

'Thank you, no. This is, I take it, the institution to which my patient has been admitted?'

'Indeed.'

Dr Parker somewhat collapses once he accepts a seat. Driving through such weather has taken more out of him than expected. Though the sobriety of an emergency roused his flesh to some cohesion, pads and chunks are beginning to sag apart. The Superintendent sees this and is intrigued.

'I can show you her last report sheet,' he offers civilly.

He reaches for the in-tray and, what's more, there it is, promptly to hand. With satisfaction and a show of efficiency he passes the limp sheet across his desk.

Patient lies in bed in a semi-stuporous condition and resists passively when made to stand up. Frequently bumps her head against the wall, though not an epileptic. Questioned about obsessional horse talk, patient states she acts under the influence of hypnotism. Her general behaviour since being under observation has been one mentally astray.

Developed delusions regarding a male nurse, Vernon Ross, claiming he 'detains me when I am well enough to be discharged' and then saying, 'I would kill him if I had a gun.'

Dr Parker reads what is before him, until, at length, the words imprint his memory. So, he sees past them and into them. He sees into the cheap paper to the point of dazzlement. Next, he assembles the massive calm of wasted years, the disappointment, the struggle through quagmires, the monumental grief for a life depleted – struck by the revelation that he has, nonetheless, upheld his principles, that he is able to embrace failure and loss because he can truly claim to have resisted any base act, anything he might be ashamed of, that he has behaved with honour in the face of his detractors and that such stiffening has delivered him intact to this purpose, this eventuality, this epiphany compounded of loss: his own and that of the strange little woman in his care.

'I shall not insist on seeing her where she is kept, nor doing what she is made to do.'

'?'

'She can be brought here to me, if you like.'

Bevis Radcliffe shakes off his melancholy and his welcome.

'I fear you are under some misapprehension, Dr Parker. Lorna may have been your patient prior to being admitted. In this place, she is my inmate. As Superintendent,' he elaborates (and is immediately grateful to the Department for his more modest title), 'I have charge of her care. Whether you – or anybody else – may see her is for me to decide. No sooner had you put your signature to the committal than you passed her over to me. There's no going back on that, I fear. She has ceased to be a mere medical case.'

'Mr Radcliffe,' the doctor checks the name on the

brass desk-plate as he uses it for the first time, 'I believe you might be interested to know that I signed no such document.'

This single rock dropped in a deep still pool instantly sets ramifications travelling, the disturbances soon to become all-comprehending. The Superintendent waits to be told more.

'She was fetched behind my back,' the old man rumbles on, 'and without my knowledge.'

'She had been consulting you?'

'Indeed, she was about to begin treatment for chronic depression, a condition which, as you may or may not know,' (he checks the brass plate again, in case it clarifies whether *mister* might indicate the rank of surgeon) 'can be treated. Perhaps not cured or reversed but treated and, almost certainly, alleviated with a tricyclic antidepressant. Pardon me if I am elucidating the obvious.'

The ripples continue to agitate the pool, expanding and expanding.

'Will you excuse me a moment?'

The Superintendent half turns his back and confides in the phone.

'Vernon? Have Mrs Shoddy brought to my office, please. Immediately ... well, in that case, as soon as possible.'

Noiselessly he replaces the handset while some monstrous premonition seizes him. He explains.

'They need to check which work party she is on. Everything having been thrown into chaos today ...'

love without hope

This chaos he identifies by indicating the window, the torrential rain and the street itself a turbulent cataract. Even now, a baby's pram topples over to be washed sidelong down the gutter. He leaps up to stare out, wiping condensation from the pane, needing to be certain the pram is empty. As it surely is, slewing past below, already clogged with leaves and waterlogged. The visitor, from where he sits, cannot see but, at last, he surrenders the report sheet he has been shown, letting it drift across the polished desk.

The hectic din of gurgling, trickling, pounding and a monotonous purling that both whispers and roars, neither swells nor diminishes. From somewhere deep within the building a door bangs. Moments later, voices float up the stairwell, only to remain suspended there in the sickening hollow of an emergency. Electric alarm bells begin jangling out in the yard, bells on every building, bells with an unvarying volume, relentless as the deluge itself. A motor can be faintly heard starting up. The office door opens, though no one has knocked. The Superintendent's secretary silently appears, poking her head around, grimacing at him behind the visitor's back, miming urgency and waving a folded piece of paper.

Nurse Felicity wakes to the embers of a dream – just in time to fan them back to life – an inspired dream in which she has discovered that the poor creatures she cares for cannot help the way they are. That's it. Yes, because they're surrounded by swarming maggots. In the excitable and powerful clarity of almost-waking the truth dawns on her. The inmates *contracted* their madness. Caught it from someone else.

That's what's new.

So, contrary to everything nurses are taught, they should be treated as victims of an epidemic, no more culpable than sufferers from smallpox or flu. At one stroke she has seen past mere symptoms to the very origin of their insanity. She will be thanked. She will be famous. She will change everything. These are not flawed people, nor even deluded people, they are simply unlucky: having caught the bug from the lip of a shared tea cup, perhaps, or from a blowfly settling on them, one day, all unnoticed. And now she suspects their food is contaminated by a plague of insomnia. Just how such contagions can be passed on will be the subject of clandestine enquiries in her semi-dream. She promises. Yet she dare not let any colleagues know, or even suspect, not until she has absolute proof. So, she must work quickly and talk to the patients, avid as she is for more detail. Being a scientist in the field. The epileptics will be good ones to start on, the *petit mal* sufferers, who spend much of their time rationally coherent. And while researching new cases she can reach back into her fully sleeping dream to fish up items of illness to match... transmissions by contaminated water in the case of delirium (she must be careful to boil her own supplies for drinking), meat or poultry carrying neurasthenia and so forth. How deaf the whole staff has been to the truth! Patients forever complain 'something tastes funny in my food' leading to outright claims of being poisoned. Perhaps they are! Poor things being bitten by mosquitoes carrying catatonic stupor, sneezes spreading paranoia. There is no end to it, quite apart from ordinary words and the damage words can do, words with horrid consequences for those already suffering straggles and gorges ... through the closed curtains of her daylight sleep Nurse Felicity now anticipates the full catastrophe: the hospital as nothing more nor less than a quarantine station. The quarantine station comprising the Court of Lunacy, the wards, working kitchens and laundry, the flowerbeds bright with impatiens, the eternal clock and its herniated bell exposed, dissected lawns and arterial gravelways as the whole place crawls with maggots. Pestilence everywhere. Diseased maggots drop out of ceiling vents. Maggots emerge from stewpots to wriggle across the lino. Everywhere she goes she sees them. She treads on them, cushioned, as one might tread on gum. Maggots fall from moist lips and from wax-laden ears. In her dream she rushes to the nearest sink to scrub up, she scrubs her hands three times over, as if on duty in an operating theatre, as protection against the swarming epilepsy and as protection against infection by Julie, in particular, having risked putting her fingers in Julie's mouth when she was woken in the middle of her sleep to help the poor thing ... So, like an Indian missionary tending leprosy sufferers, she's advised to be as careful as she is compassionate. The seeking eyes of the afflicted defy her best efforts because, in some place deep within their helplessness, they feel rage. They lust for revenge. Well, why not? They have been misunderstood all their lives and what other revenge is within their power? So, of course, they're glad that their portion of hurt can be passed on and shared. They are dangerous. Yes.

love without hope

She herself ought not to risk catching the madness.

Opportunity knocks. Felicity, aware that this is medical heresy, knows perfectly well what her colleagues will say. As is the case with all visionaries who refuse to be gagged by the system. So now – the knocking persists and someone calls out to her – she alone must carry the full shock of – the caller says something about Lorna going absent. 'Lorna is contagious,' she mumbles, 'I was on night shift last night.' Lorna will spread her delusions of innocence out there among the unsuspecting daylight public. More knocking. She wakes with a start. Weeks previously, when, for reasons now superseded, Felicity dared contact the doctor who signed Lorna's committal, he had referred her to a fellow nurse, Olga Ostrov by name. She sinks back on the pillow. Following that phone call she and Olga had exchanged letters, one each, so it's not too soon to say Olga is a friend, though they may never meet. The voice comes again, 'Lorna has . . .' In Felicity's dream, which she fans back into flame, she even dares – as she would never dare with Vernon – share her radical idea. Olga does not yet reply.

The knocking resumes, more urgently. Then she hears the emergency bell. Still fuddled and reluctant to get up, she reaches out to part the heavy curtains. Only to recoil from the sight of a million silver bullets streaking at her window.

Gail, who can put two and two together, does not know what to do about it. Her husband left the girls in charge of the shop and drove to the local airport. This much Russell explained, mouth vigorously at work on an egg and bacon roll, words washed down with hasty gulps of tea, and he even presented himself for her assurance that he looked his best. He looked – now she comes to think of it – shady. His tight collar too tight, his suit too creaseless, his tie too loud. She even caught him spraying the interior of the Toyota with Aeroguard before he drove off into the rain.

love without hope

She can put the pieces together like a child's building blocks: Rita's indignation at being chased off (besides being actually hit at) by Mrs Shoddy wielding a broom, the Public Trustee taking over Mrs Shoddy's affairs, Olga suddenly discovering she has the deposit she couldn't afford before. She thinks and thinks. The same factors, the same coincidences. But she cannot reach a decision. Her body delays the process while being transmogrified into the froglike bloodlessness of guilt – because she has also played a part – her flesh cold and her suckered fingertips sticking to things. Proof comes whilst she is out in the laundry filling a glass vase for the bunch of rosebuds he has bought for the occasion. In detaching her fingers, she drops the vase. Like a miniature explosion, shards shoot away across the floor, spinning and glimmering. She stares helplessly down at them, the mishap resonating with that secret shock of accusation. Only now does she remember that she is supposed to attend the funeral of dear old Elsie Southwell who died of a heart attack though everyone thought she would last to a hundred. Right this minute workmen with shovels will be burying the coffin.

Baking smells clog the kitchen. She has been told to cook a meal, to have the house perfect for an important guest and then keep out of sight. The hoovering and scrubbing, the polishing and cushion-plumping are complete. Just as she collects her wits and stoops down with dustpan and brush to sweep up the damage, she hears the Toyota drive into the carport. She leaves the dustpan on the floor with the shattered glass. She snatches a china vase from the cupboard instead and sticks the flowers in without wasting time on water. She steps out, crushing brittle bits underfoot, shuts the door on her disaster, crosses the kitchen and places the rosebuds on the hall stand just inside the front door at the exact moment when Russell slots his key in and his approaching voice is suddenly a notch louder as the dog scampers ahead of him.

'. . . which is why we can't be seen hurrying.'

She darts into the bedroom and closes the door, listening at the crack.

'Is there something I don't know?' a man's voice cavils.

'Not that I can think of. Please come in.'

Nothing but a little matter of wrecking someone's life! Gail thinks.

'Russell, this smells good,' the stranger says.

'We'll just grab a bite to eat and then we can be off. The place is a fair way out of town. Secluded, you might say. And with a view to kill for. Oh, and my wife sends her apologies.'

Gail hears the oven door open, the cutlery and dishes. She entertains the idea that there is nothing to stop her stepping out, right into her own diningroom, and telling the stranger the whole truth, insofar as she understands it. And that's far enough, all said and done.

The BMW leaves the last street of houses and the last of the bitumen behind. Dr Parker looks back. But the mental hospital is as invisible as the hill it stands on. He drives ahead, probing his way toward a five-ways junction of dirt roads. He makes his choice. Proceeding slowly, he peers into the fields on either side. Another half-kilometre and, the car having crept to a halt, he climbs out. Cursing his damaged eyesight, leaning on the walking stick, he straightens himself to call her name.

'Lorna!'

Nothing. He tramps around, caught up in a turmoil of

perplexity. He'd been too alarmed to wait for any explanation as to how she might have got out: and made the simple assumption that an escaping person always prefers downhill to uphill. So, as he himself left the asylum, he turned toward the bridge over the creek. A flash flood already streaming across the roadway, one of the onlookers shouted out, warning him that the whole thing might go at any moment. Without hesitation, he put the car into second and cruised through, a bow-wave surging on either side. Once across, he stopped a moment to speak to a woman who thought she might know the vagrant he was enquiring about, having shared a smile and an umbrella with her a short while back.

It gives him hope. He knows he must find her before the mental hospital staff can capture her again. He must. Any delay could cost her survival. Archibald Parker reaches into his malady of a bungled life, into his lack of sleep, calling to order the focus of tired eyes, assembles the qualities necessary to a hunter, the alertness required for stalking, for bagging the quarry before younger fitter rivals. Because they will be on her trail already. No question.

Peering into the rain, windscreen wipers thrashing, his window down, he thinks of those rivals with a hatred compounded of respect for their superiority at the sport and loathing. That poor little shred of a person is so far out of luck as to have no one on her side more adequately equipped than he. And he recalls how she once fled his surgery rather than hear his advice on managing her condition. Neglecting to pay, which was so unlike her and which he would never have the heart to draw to her attention. That afternoon he had walked through the waiting room, shaking his already shaky head, and marvelled aloud (for the benefit of his receptionist) that the lady was so forgetful she left money on his desk instead of asking for a receipt. 'Make it out just the same,' he'd said, 'then she can collect it when she next comes in.' And paid from his own pocket the price of a bottle of Gilbey's.

So, having shouted himself hoarse, he returns to the five-ways junction.

He has one advantage: he knows her. And he knows she is sane, a countrywoman who will make intelligent choices. For a start, she won't stick to any road. He has to choose – as she would – access to the best-looking cover. His heart frets at the thought of her, her dwindled state, her nerveless hands, her pitiful frailty, mustering strength to stagger away through this wild weather. What did they do to her in there? Shudders hold him together. He will find her and take her home. He will kidnap her if necessary . . . and be damned to the consequences. From now on they'll have to deal with *him*.

He negotiates the slippery road, thickets on either side thinning for pastures to open out ahead. He has plenty of experience driving in such conditions. This is familiar enough. He scarcely notices. The windscreen wipers thrash swiftly back and forth. His vision sharpening and his concentration resurrected, he organises his ruined brain for the task of coming to a decision. He stops again to lower the window and shout among the last patches of scrub, imagining her crouched there. Nothing. Already exhausted with hallooing, his ribs ache. He gets out for a better view. He calls and calls in his ragged voice, startling a flock of galahs so they screech around his head. Water drips from the brim of his hat, his shoes are sodden and his trousers flap against his legs. He opens his umbrella. He fights off despair. Resting to catch his breath and for the knotted ball of his heart to relax, he finds everything distilled to a final showdown between the will and the flesh. Each detail essential. A band strapped around his chest tightens when he breathes. He knows he must be careful. He diagnoses angina. Yet his will, lawlessly fixed and single-minded, urges him on. Heedless of cost or risk. Never mind the rain. Rain is the least of it and no more than a hampering vexation. What can it matter that his suit is soaked and a dribble inside his collar – delicate and disquieting as an unidentified insect – trickles down to explore his back?

At each new stop-off place, having surveyed the land, discounting sheep and deducting cattle but never catching sight of her, he heaves his wreck of flesh back to the warm dry car, turns up the heating, breathes a blast from the demister and sets his wheels creeping another stage into the lustrous obscurity. She cannot have got far, puny confused little thing that she is. Surely, she cannot even have got as far as this? Perhaps he should turn back.

love without hope

Yes, to try a different track. Why hadn't he given this one up before? Wasting precious time! Sheer stubbornness. Ridiculous! Irresponsible! Furiously, he spins the wheel to send the BMW hurtling too fast back the way he has come, almost to the beginning of the built-up area. Briefly, he catches a ghostly glimpse of the mental hospital away to his left, while slewing into a Y-bend and angling off at a northerly tangent. He misjudges the road. Tyres slither along the shoulder. As he stamps on the brake his shoe slips momentarily and the car lurches. But he has it under control. He slows down.

On the lookout once again, Dr Parker proceeds deliberatively collectedly across the scrutinised country, paying heed neither to eye-strain nor the whispers in his head. Billows of rain have begun thinning across an open plain to lift from the undulant grassland horizon. Whispers whisper. He hears but cannot understand. The rain has been smudged green by the pastures, the saturated green of rampant succulence. Mist begins gathering on the oozing land. There is nowhere here for a fugitive to take cover. Except – except in the mist itself! The whispers grow so insistent he must stop again to get out. Rain gives way to an eerie mizzle. Not much point bothering about the umbrella. He leaves it, seizing his walking stick instead. He shakes his great shaggy head and even bangs one ear. Down to business, Dr Parker stares behind, before and to either side. He calls and calls.

Something about this place jogs his memory. He comes on a cattle trough and a gate. He opens the gate, going through and shutting it after him. Some notion speaks to him. He waits, listening to the light. Yes, he has it: a memory of Lorna Shoddy's own paddocks, much like this, give or take proximity to the ocean. A similar breast-like hill. A reminiscent approach. Underfoot, the spongy ground feels alive, it rises or sinks unequally, creature of his subconscious, as he boosts his asymmetrical clumsiness where his blind will dictates. The wet has him skidding a bit and his skeleton aches with the effort of maintaining balance. His throat is raw. Pressure crushes his chest. Yet, recklessly he forges on, the weight of a continent clinging to his boots. Numbed and gasping, he trudges to the limit, till he fetches up against that yielding damp.

He can slog no further. So, the departing storm abandons the wreckage of his hulk right there in the middle of a field, as a perpendicular craggy intrusion lodged in space, lichened and already weathering to a monument. He begins to erode. The world moves on. And the moving world brings changes, gradually tearing the mists apart as frayed tatters till he espies a tiny figure up ahead in the distance, a hazy charcoal thumbprint of a figure, at the far rim of the fence-line. He shakes his head to get it clear. Yes. And blood instantly floods his heart. The articulated parts of his body cohere. An ancient energy burning against the resistance of decay, he assembles himself to bellow:

'Lorna! Lorna!'

Forlorn syllables, each in turn gagged by muffling

love without hope

damp and muffling earth and the muffling sagging cloud. He labours again to truck himself her way, though the grip of soil holds him back and his hindered feet delay him. Yet he rouses himself to the ambling gait of an elephant. Even, for a brief few steps, with walking stick flashing wetly, lunging into a trot. Oh, his heart! The pain won't let him breathe. Yet, he sees she has been stopped by the fence. He might, he just might . . . desperately driving on, he gets her clearer.

'Lorna!'

She hears nothing but the music of eternity, her feet already buried in grass.

'*Lor-na!*'

She seems to be seeking a stile or a gap. He watches her falter and slant away from the barbed wire. Then . . . then the moment comes. She notices him. Though still a fair way off, he perceives her shock, a shock that seizes hold and shakes her, repulsing her and casting her twisted form aside.

But doesn't she recognise him? Surely?

Mrs Shoddy comes to herself with a jolt. Now and now only does she concede that he has her cornered. Terror, right here in the flesh, closes in as a lumberous hulk armed with a stick for beating her. She sees him thrash at the ground with it. Recoiling, she watches the massive effort expended by his hunched form to get her. Nearer, his hand reaching through the grain of scratched air – big as Vernon's hand – he pauses a mere minute away. The screws on her terror tighten. Where to flee? Terrible shouts clubbing her ear, her whole being winces at the impact. The music she has been part of comes to an abrupt end. He bellows. Only at the third and fourth repetitions does she realise these bellowings take the shape of her name. Well, that confirms it! He knows her. It is her he's pursuing. He has come for her, though this is not Vernon. And he has caught her. She cannot escape his funeral clothing, his funeral hat. His cheeks so red with rage.

Next thing, his steaming breaths already suffocate her and his prehensile fury is about to entrap and abduct her, even as she sinks to the ground. She will die. Death is the force she feels tossing her aside. Her mind struggles to comprehend, while her hand (perhaps with some memory of God's last gift to her when she came upon the miracle pliers in just such grass as this at home) gropes round her, searching but encountering only a liquefied pat of dung. Some other animal has been here before her. And this is what she holds up to fend off the executioner, this tiny ineffectual shit-covered palm. Even while, monstrously imminent over her, he is a creature whose fury renders him bereft of the power of speech. There will be no mercy.

The last of the music sinks around them. The mist swirls as he subsides to his knees. The unravelled harmonies of rain forsake her, leaving nothing to buoy her up, revealing the world as entirely earthbound, composed of pattering drops and the grunts of a pursuer

love without hope

whose face is buried between his knees – presenting his back as a vast ball, as something evolved for rolling, for flattening and smashing things down – in preparation for the final assault.

When he speaks she will learn what he intends for her punishment.

Yet he has dropped the stick. And this slender object lies to one side, the silver knob lambent among beaded blades. And ... and she knows it. This one familiar detail. Having noticed it periodically over the span of many years. It takes her back to the time she suffered from flu, the time of tonsillitis, the time of a broken arm when good old Archie Parker travelled all the way out to the farm on a house call to set the bone for her. She reaches her tiny claw for the stick, even as he unfolds his face to reveal what is hidden and presents the moon of it toward her. So, she recognises him, her own doctor, already dead, turning her way moments after he expels his last breath in a plea for recognition. Long moments, his eyes are held by hers. His fear by hers.

'Archie,' she whispers in awe.

Then his head nods forward once, forward, to fold down again on his chest, snugly into the hollow created for it, the chest itself double-folding against his knees and only then – slow as a house tipped by an earthquake – he rolls on his side in the squelch. She knows death when she sees it. She lets her index finger trace the bridge of his noble nose to collect the drop at the tip and draw a shining mark across the sad bags of his lifeless cheek.

'Archie, dear Archie,' Mrs Shoddy whispers, her whole heart suddenly flooded with radiance. 'Thank you for coming.'

Propped up in bed on the pillows of a migraine, Rita Gibbons figures it all out. The cheque has arrived. Well and good. But the shock of such a large amount agitates her. Hundreds and hundreds. She can't bring herself to bank it. Meanwhile, with a furtive sense of accomplishment, she hides it safely under the tray where she keeps the waterglass for her teeth. No one ever touches that. The truth is that she is terrified of what her husband will say. For the first time in her married life she is unhappy, simply because she might be found out. She feels she's on the back foot. Already she has started asking his opinion about this and that. She even lets him make decisions, though his discomfort and surprise are obvious. But she can't help herself. As for accepting any such windfall and going ahead with the plan of adding it to her nest-egg, somehow the magnitude of her good luck spoils all that.

Still, why shouldn't she have the benefit?

Toothless and bedridden, the one thing she regrets is that, in her official capacity, she did what the voice on the telephone asked her to do and paid Olga a visit, reporting the state of Lorna Shoddy's house – no doubt he was concerned about her, with him living somewhere else and all. Simple. And there was no reason for discussing it with Gail Savage.

Rita has the elements sorted. At least as far as her involvement is concerned. What *Olga* might have to do with it doesn't bear thinking about. There are already more facts than one could hope to know how to manage: she lets the pain get to work cushioning them so they have less weight but (and it's the mystery of headaches) no less clarity. The long and short of it is that some wealthy man – for whatever reason – wants Lorna cared for. And he needs it done by the book. By a proper medical assessment. So he approaches someone. Someone local. As a senior citizen and longstanding President of the CWA, who better than herself? The truth is that she and Gail *were* shocked at finding that house in a state not fit for human habitation. So, all she did was to report the fact. The later messages were something else.

Yes, yes, Mrs Gibbons agrees with herself, gums slapping. It's obvious. And, once Olga felt obliged to pass on her own concerns to the doctor, either she or he would have faced the task, no doubt, of speaking to the shire. Or the Health Department. Or both. Most likely through a local councillor. A flash of surprise and pain wipes out her bedroom and bed, her clothes hung on the wardrobe door, the rumpled eiderdown and the dressing table mirror. Lies. They were all lies! She knows, now, what the cheque is for. How could she have been such a fool! She rolls herself to the edge of the bed so her feet can be let down to the carpet. She cranks herself to a seated position. The waterglass in which her teeth are soaking rocks perilously as she fumbles for that cheque. She stares once more at the unbelievable sum written there before she rips the fragile slip of paper in half and in half again. And rips the bits yet again. Viciously ripping. Desolation overwhelms her.

'But I knew her dad, old Jack Boswell, the drunk,' she blubbers. 'I wouldn't do this, if that's what this is. Wickedness, I call it.'

Recklessly driven, the institution van hurtles along the dirt, Vernon at the wheel. The asylum janitor, having abandoned that problem furnace, sits attentively beside him, on the lookout. Having passed a BMW parked at the roadside with its headlights and blinker still on, they recognise it, scream to a halt and back up. Both men jump down. But they find no one inside, though the engine is still running and the windscreen wipers sweep this way and that.

They peer across smudged country, able to make out very little, certainly nothing worth stopping for. Though

love without hope

the rain is lightening off, a mist – already obscuring the far fence – drags its belly nearer. For a fleeting lapse, Vernon is catapulted back to childhood and his childhood fear of some shapeless alien, an alien he thought he'd forgotten, an intelligence described as too huge to have definite limits, a compound, a colony, loosely held together in the shape of an aerial squid, proceeding blimp-like, but so soft and so swiftly proliferating it didn't notice bits tearing off against the ground while its malignant unopposable body spread to take over the world. He shakes his head to clear it.

He opens the BMW's door and flips the wipers and the blinker off because they irritate him. And then the motor. After a moment's indecision, he leaves the keys in the ignition. Not his responsibility. Placing one hand on the seat, he finds it warm. He unfolds himself as he backs his body out into the drizzle again. Then, upright, favours the janitor with a mystified shrug. But already the cogs are engaging, he is matching clues. Now he retraces the car's tracks to read certain sharp skid marks in the mud. Evidently the old man had jammed on his brakes, so *he* must have seen something. The afternoon begins to fail from lack of sky. Vernon hunts the ground for more signs and finds a footprint. Deeply marked. Size twelve at least. He examines it. Also the direction the shoe took: going that way, through a gate, toward the bank of mist. Though he can see nothing over there, other than wallowing vapour sleep-swimming his way, he sets off. Wordlessly, the janitor follows. A good reliable bloke, this janitor. They unlatch the gate and stride in across the paddock.

Coming upon a linen handkerchief in the grass, a man's handkerchief, the two pursuers press on into the thick of a glaucous dome whorling around them . . . only to be brought up short by an unaccountable noise. Standing motionless, they listen. A kind of repetitive tearing and a blanket-folding sound being flop-folded again . . . and now again. Then snuffling snorts and the breath of some huge soft comfortable routine. They listen together, hair standing up along their arms. This is no human presence. There is an accompaniment of curiously liquid shufflings, too, interrupted by an occasional cough. Pushing on through lush grass, they strain to see. Neither speaks. It could not possibly be the elderly country doctor, surely? Unless doing something unimaginable. No. They share a premonition: this goes beyond the human.

All at once, before their amazed eyes, an ambling boulder approaches. Still vague, with faintly rumbled comments on its own locomotion, the monster emerges. They identify it as a black bull. The bull grazes even while it proceeds, planting each massive leg before moving another, hoofs swishing and squelching in the wet grass, tail flicking periodically, nose snuffling into the wet ground, bulwarks of muscle mounding across shoulder and haunch, neck wattles pendant, huge testicles swinging and (probably the most alarming aspect of all) penis beginning to show a pink extension. The animal, knowing they are there in its path, ponders their intrusion. Its tiny black eyes on them, it comes hushing forward, forging through the silage, indifferent as a mythological beast, last of its kind, contemplating some vision beyond loneliness, with the total confidence of being larger than any other animal it has ever encountered.

The two men back away, keeping a check on those short sharp horns glittering with varnish. The creature – nostrils busily collecting interpretations – approaches unswervingly, destined to follow the set path of an ancient story which must be told over and over without deviation. They hang on to their nerve, not daring to bolt, knowing there is no cover anyhow (no tree, no fence) within running distance. Thus, the black bull looms colossally close – driving a cloud of warmth – still cropping grass and indulging, now and then, in a bit more tail-flicking. Impossible to anticipate what messages might be activating angers in that woolly head. All the while they are held by its watchful eye. They boggle, paralysed by fear as, step by step, the dreaming monster approaches and then ... passes by. Just like that. Its progress utterly undisturbed. So, already, the danger goes ambling away, beyond them, harmlessly – no doubt carrying their image in memory – and plods off into the mist. Ambles, luxuriating in a slick of rain and the succulent provisions, a touch of elegance about its ankles, an almost rakish tilt to its hindquarters (as they now see while exhaling, at last), propelling itself majestically into obscurity. And, as it goes, the bull tows the bulk of the mist with it, dragging a veil off the thinning disclosures of the paddock. Rain begins to fall more purposefully again as delicate vapours rend, trail and dissipate in still air. The green of earth intensifies. While underfoot the unrolling ground – being unrolled – extends the width of a gradual incline. Tasselled curtains continue to part on a disappointing tableau. Away ahead, scarcely above ground level and masked by dripping thistles, two insignificant half-buried figures form a pietà, the grieving female made tiny by grief, the male prostrate, as if resting in her lap somehow distances him from her, embodying the stillness of a shared moment. And nothing else in the world exists.

This is how things appear, but it cannot be right. Because Vernon and his companion, as pursuers, seem to be neither expected nor feared.

Next thing, in one flip of time, they find themselves right at the scene. But, confronted by Mrs Shoddy's delicate gesture of compassion, her cradling of the corpse's face, the janitor finds himself arrested by the beauty he sees before him. And Vernon, still treading into childhood and discomfited by the strangeness of this, gets swept deeper and even farther back among his memories. At the same moment as his mind victoriously surveys his quarry, his body finds itself blocked (though he cannot nail the feeling) by some taboo surviving from infancy. He gazes. The look on that starveling female's face, convulsed with cold and afflicted with trembling as

love without hope

she is, baffles interpretation. Is it composure or anguish?

The janitor takes up Dr Parker's silver-topped cane and tests the feel of it in his hand. Knowing better than to touch one of the inmates, he stands aside for the man with training. Vernon must decide what is to be done. But Mrs Shoddy already hears the cellophane world collapsing, the alarm of small lives around her, clicking carapaces and whisking feathers, and from somewhere down the slope, from the heart of the mist, a mournful bellow. Once or twice she had sensed just such an impending beast move among her horses, she and they intuiting the selfsame alarm. And on each occasion, sure enough, death would trample among them to electrify the air with foreboding. It was never far away. Now her native cunning speaks out of the despair of recapture.

'I got lost in the rain,' she explains.

Oh yes, she recognises her enemy, she knows all right, she knows his name (already she can read the stitching on his tunic) and she gets his measure. She has escaped his element and reached her own. She has dared. She has found a way, thanks to the opportunity offered by Julie, she has come, she has proved there is still a world of paddocks and livestock, of hope, of courage and compassion. She is the richer for Archie Parker's gift. Archie believed in her. He believed in her so much he risked and lost his life. She cannot let him down. She takes all these gifts into her heart. She will not give the asylum bullies an excuse to brutalise her further. No more than she can help.

'I can't find my way.'

The watchers watch, seeking signs of a crack in her tale, a giveaway symptom of hysteria, the least artifice. She shudders in her rag of sodden clothes and murmurs through blue lips:

'I am so tired.'

The catalogue begins to come. Doddering, she spins it out as she sneezes and gasps.

'Turning and turning, never seeing anything. The rain. The fog. Nothing anywhere here . . .'

And she squints about her, as they do, at the undulant pastures under undulant, lifting cloud.

'Could you,' she pleads, to finish it off, 'show me somewhere warm?'

Vernon says not a word. He signals his companion to take the doctor's feet while he hoists the old man's shoulders. Mrs Shoddy wipes the shit from her hand and accepts the walking stick being offered her by the janitor. She is not sure who he is, but she takes it gladly. She will treasure this as Archie's own. Now the three of them set off across bull-haunted territory, back the way they came, burdened with the tremendous affliction of an angry corpse.

The corpse grows prodigious. Dr Parker already weighs them down, these two strong men, he makes himself inert, massier than flesh and bone. He has them staggering. They drag and drop him and he grows ever more bloated and leaden, so they have difficulty even raising him off the ground again, his boots slippery, his

love without hope

thin hair greasy, the hat they place on his chest rolling off as he mounds himself huger, ampler and super-solid. They lift but he sinks. They lose their footing and he escapes their grip. They wrestle him and he makes no resistance. Like ponderous rubber he thwarts their efforts. They sweat, quietly cursing, stertorous with frustration, groaning at the strain. One of his shoes slips off, his leg trails and needs to be hoisted up, his fingernails rake at the ground for purchase against them. His determination of a corpse cannot be beaten or persuaded out of him. He is fixed in it, hampering them, until at last Mrs Shoddy herself feels it.

She perceives what she could never have imagined: Archie Parker has them in his power. He is now the one to decide. They are panting and straining. Archie makes himself a whale, bulbous black and wet, cumbersome and recalcitrant. His skill is incomprehensible to the likes of such people and he knows it. Not to her. She obeys his instructions and walks ahead, as if blind, feeling her choices with the stick. And they will follow once they succeed in heaving the fat hard gripless smoothness of the dead doctor up out of the treacherous grass. She grows lighter with a fever he has prescribed, finding her way down the slope through breaking ravines of mist. Even as they abandon their attempt to carry the corpse and begin dragging him, one to each foot, he skives to one side then the other, his shoulders swing to meet the tide of progress like a corpulent figurehead and they must stop to right him.

She is a long way in front when the mist begins backing up behind her. She can see two vehicles at the verge of the road. She keeps going. The distance between her and her captors widens as, heaving with bafflement, they stop to puzzle out a solution. The body lies face down between them, arms spread defiantly to hold them back. She is as good as alone. She is, with Archie's stick, alone. She is as alone as she was during the deluge when she walked into the music. Except that this time the aloneness is on a rim of silence, an arc of some gigantic breast, some heaving of the land which reminds her of home. She knows this country. She knows paddocks like these and the terrain of the four-footed. She meets with a benign bull dragging some mist uphill behind him. She approaches and runs her hand along his withers as he passes. He swings his massive head a moment her way, neck compacted on itself, before returning to graze – a contented grumbling in his chest – ears swinging wide, attentively, and a shag of grass dangling from his lip. He lets some dung go with a *plop plop plop plop-plop plop*. On she pushes, her progress a rhythm now, the stick her aid. The doctor's car stands by the road. Once, she looks behind her (though wondering in that moment whether this might be the one forbidden vanity) in time to see the bull pilot himself round to face the intruders from the asylum, to see him glower and plant his cogitative belligerence in their path, to see him baulk at the curious sight of a trespassing dead body that grasps two living bodies by the hand.

love without hope

The mist envelops them. This is enough. She need not hurry.

Mrs Shoddy heads for the gate, left open by some ignorant person. Lightly she goes, quite unaware how she stumbles and sinks and struggles like a bird with a broken wing, how she slips and cants, to all appearances, desperately. No, she feels it as a gift, her passage. From back there, as if in some echoing minotaur-chamber, comes the mighty hollow resonance of the bull's roar. Once out through the gate, she shuts it behind her and latches the chain on to the peg.

She has only once been in Archie's nice car and that was five years ago, when her Land Rover broke down and he gave her a lift to the town garage. But she knows it, and knows it is his. She's not interested in the hospital van. She ushers herself into the BMW. She turns the key in the ignition. Tut-tut, he had not put the handbrake on. She lets the lovely thing roll out on to the dirt road (she should buy one like it), a road pitted with potholes. Her sort of road. There is still enough daylight to see. Archie's warning voice forbids her to use the headlamps. Not yet. A rush of deliciously warmed air circulates round her. She finds herself in heaven. Just where she hopes *he* is – as he surely is – not just because he's her saviour but because he was . . . who he was. She allows the road to unravel behind her.

The tank is nearly full. She accepts the mystery of a marked way to guide how she goes and, at the first turning offered, turns. Well, you don't look a gift horse.

So, this is how she will enjoy the world's freedoms. At the very next intersection she turns again, driving at her usual twenty kilometres an hour, through patches of dispersing mist and gentle rain. As Mrs Shoddy drives, the world bursts into light and closes away in darkness, the sun makes a late wan appearance before being blotted out by another heavy shower. She gets the wipers working and reaches to turn on the radio. A bass voice, already tuned in, sings unbelievably deep notes. Indulging in a little lilt of vanity, she places it as Russian.

'You see,' she pipes aloud to herself, 'I can't be mad.'

Chriostos woskresie, sings the bass. A man, she assures herself, and such a man. She knows this as one of the beautiful moments of her life. Keeping the sunset behind her, she heads east. She can now switch on the headlamps as she drives – turning alternately left and right – weaving her way across her beloved country, warming up and drying out, driving to nowhere but in the general direction of love. She thinks about Archie and, in the midst of life, the mystery of death: this idea has its own music quite different from the music on the radio, but every bit as sombre and magnificent. *She* is in the midst of life, she now sees the truth. She is not dead. Her awful sufferings are a measure of how intensely alive she is. Because she has survived.

She finds a packet of cashew nuts in the glovebox and this gives her something forgotten to chew. The night welcomes her and a curious thought visits her that, supposing her bull (for so she thinks of him) chose his

love without hope

colour for the usual reason of camouflage, he must be a friend of the night and all the more threatening to his enemies after dark. She can still hear his obsessive ripping of grass. High beam makes lovely lace of the evening trees. And shadows begin to dance around her, enlivened by skittish kangaroos veering out of the way (with plenty to spare because it's her and not some speeding ignoramus), so that she must sometimes catch her breath at the beauty of it all.

The janitor reaches out a restraining hand to prevent Vernon from making any rash move. The bull plants itself in their path, tentacles of mist snaking around its shoulders and belly. They start backing away, so very slowly they scarcely seem to move at all, leaving the corpse abandoned between themselves and the beast. So, they retreat – step by creeping step – with the benefit of a dead body as decoy. But the disobliging weather begins to clear so that a single glance over their shoulders is enough for them to see that the fence where they found the doctor is too far away to be reached with safety. Even supposing they split up, only one would make it. And they agree upon this in the flicker of an eye. Best to shuffle away together, slowly, slowly, while the going's good, though clamped in the vice-like teeth of terror.

The bull, having seen enough, steps forward, the tonnage of each footfall counterbalanced by the sway of his head.

The two men keep pace, slow-footing it in reverse back up the hill, mesmerised. So, the brute, coming upon the intervention of Dr Parker, allows several minutes to accumulate while the corpse in its wet black suit is assessed – a corpse so powerful and perfectly unafraid as to outface him, unyielding and motionless. The majestic creature snuffles closer, drawn to investigate. Next, as if smacked on the snout, the bull recoils fractionally, his monumental head packed with the weightiest of all recognitions. Rocking his burden back on tremendous haunches, he withdraws one step. Another. Presents his profile, eye swivelling.

The janitor seizes on this. He takes the lead and creeps forward, sheltering behind the dead man. Vernon, despite a twinge of resentment (even in such desperate circumstances), follows. The black bull takes to ambling a short distance away, aeons of dominance investing his slowness with the majesty of law, before returning to confront the intrusion. The two men crouching behind the body roll it over, gently yes, and gently roll it. Accordingly, Dr Parker's flesh settles around his re-ordered skeleton at each stage, as if finally at rest – now on his stomach, now at rest on his back – arms flopping out like wings. So, he controls them by keeping progress slow. The bull watches this curious approach (the two living appendages of the one dead body), stretching his head forward till the line from shoulder to nose straightens, hollows and arcs up for letting out a tyrant's roar. Fear locks the men, on hands and knees, behind their protector. The grass ticks with already-fallen water and only the rotating world moves. There is still some mist down by the gate, but the weather is breaking.

'What say we rush him, shouting?' the janitor whispers.

'Are you a fucking idiot or something?'

Dr Parker's corpse, hearing this, knows he must prevent them running off and leaving him. They are the enemy. Some strategy is required to hold them to his purpose. So, of his own accord – and as gradual as nightfall – he begins to roll over on his stomach, showing them a face innocent with age, squashed cheeks sagging away from his teeth to reveal a crooked grin. Then, convincingly, as if levered the next stage by gravitation alone, he rolls again. The tailored split at the back of his coat folds open, pasted there by the wet, to reveal straining braces and an enormity of buttocks. The bull backs off a further step.

The hospital men, now they are locked into a successful strategy, get to business – on hands and knees – and, slowly, slowly, roll the odour of death down against that threatening beast, driving him off and further off, his tail swishing, his head down, belligerent eyes burning, anger unremitting, his solid club-footed retreat at no stage more than provisional. So death, in a steady advance, glistening with evening light, side-over-side, flaps a hand, then a foot in the beast's face. Death is afraid of nothing, as every creature knows in its blood. Death is unstoppable.

At the gate, Dr Parker dismisses the bull and sends it drifting away through a sea of stalks and blades to weigh the issues of its mythological business. A way being clear, his captive attendants slip the latch and stoop to lift him while, with the capriciousness of the powerful, he once more makes himself difficult to manage.

When, finally, Mrs Shoddy can drive no longer, warped road disconcertingly jumpy in her headlights, she pulls over among some trees. She takes a peep into the boot and discovers several treasures there: a medical case, a folded blanket, a little car fridge containing a bottle of gin and three bottles of tonic water, a half-finished packet of biscuits, plus a banana. She eats, she drinks, she swallows some Panadol, she switches off the music, she wraps herself in a cloud of comfort and stretches her delirium out on the back seat. She can now admit how tiny and how helpless she is. And does,

love without hope

once more proving she is sane. Time to sleep for a few hours. Then she can drive again, following her backroad logic. And once the dawn breaks she will be able to confirm her direction. This much she noticed: that, long ago, when the ambulance men dragged her out of her father's house and brought her, they drove south then west. Therefore, she must continue heading east followed by north: to reach her horses, to have that responsibility sewn up, to make arrangements for them, to honour their trust.

Sleep tips the forest trunks askew, though shocking pulsations disrupt her, sudden rushes of grief jack-hammering up through her frame. Jolted, she is in torment. Yanked up off the ribbed leather with pain, paroxysms of the Actual splitting the protective sheath to burst through her numbness. She collapses on the seat again, racked by sobs. All the humiliations she has endured coagulate and flux, she gets some hint of how thrown about an epileptic must feel, but in her case she is able to take charge. She can acknowledge having been forcibly ousted from her farm, tied down, drugged, stripped of her clothes, punished, left for days in a dark corner, bundled armless in a straitjacket, reviled as a receptacle full of filth – the catalogue mounts up into a brutalisation she recalls but cannot begin to comprehend. She cannot even credit a person twice her size surviving so much. She has no notion how long she was shut away in there. A lifetime. The nausea rises and sinks. Successive tides of retching surge through her, even while the exhausted blood begins letting her down, letting her go. She can never ... she can never ...

Love without hope – it's Martin's voice reciting her favourite poem – *as when the young bird-catcher swept off his tall hat to the Squire's own daughter* ...

By early evening the news is out. The Superintendent's desk has been cleared and a large-scale map of the surrounding countryside displayed for the four people standing round his desk to pore over: a sergeant of police, a constable, the Superintendent himself and a flustered Nurse Felicity.

'Of course, my staff may have found her already,' he says. 'But they've been gone rather a long time and I feel we can delay no more. So, we should be ready for any eventuality.'

The sergeant, having listened to this preamble, takes

over. It is his turn. He establishes his authority by providing them with an overview of the terrain, illustrating the points he makes by planting the flat of his hand here, then here, then there.

'This here is scrubby hill country. Now *this* is open farmland with quite a few homesteads and small holdings. Here's the town, speaks for itself. More open pastures over here, but somewhat bigger properties, therefore not many houses. And flat bushland here along the boundaries of a National Park, through which the river runs. Right? The main routes are the highway, which you can see for yourselves, and the other main thoroughfare crossing it at an angle here – south-east to north-west – minor roads going this way, this way, down here and over there, all of them bitumen with a good surface. Easy from our point of view. Dirt roads branching pretty much in every direction, except for a little slice of rocky outcrop angling in where you see this green patch. So, over that way – on your side, Superintendent – the tableland rises, where on my side it gently slopes towards the scarp. Clear enough? The hospital is here,' he takes a pencil and slashes a ring round it, making his opinion plain. 'Our starting point. Okay. Now, am I correct in assuming the escaped person is on foot?'

'Yes,' the nurse contributes, 'and I don't think she can have gone far. Poor thing is very weak.'

The sergeant nods and returns to the map. The constable looks up.

'What's she wearing on her feet?'

love without hope

'Canvas shoes.'

'Does she know the district?' the top of the sergeant's head asks. He clarifies it, '*Did* she know the district before she was ... if you see what I mean, brought here?'

'Hard to say.' The Superintendent scratches his head. 'Her home was more than a hundred and fifty kilometres away. But whether she might have had some knowledge from before that ...'

They scan the options, as if with Mrs Shoddy's eyes, planning the most convenient route for her to take, looking for what might best suit her escape.

'The town would be no good,' the sergeant suggests. 'Sooner or later someone would bring her in, or at least report her. Bound to. So, let's not worry about that. The hill country is possible, though hard to get to and I don't think she could make it by nightfall. This farming district is all fenced in, so she'd have to stick to the road, one road or another. With a couple of police cars we could quickly cover that sector and I'm inclined to set that up without further delay. Then we've narrowed down the options. We're left with the downs country and the National Park. This is where we'll concentrate our efforts and in that order. Right?'

'I agree, sir,' the young constable offers brightly.

The Superintendent concludes the agreement by bringing them fully up to date on the hospital's own alert.

'We've sent two of our vehicles out already, one in either direction. Then there's her family doctor who called in to see her. He took himself off, too. Maybe he's had some luck.'

'Name?'

'Archibald Parker.'

'Driving?'

'A black BMW.'

The police replace their caps and they're back in business.

'That about wraps it up. The routine search can scour the roadsides north and west. We forget about the town. But we need men on the ground in these areas – south and east. How many can you muster from your staff?'

'Probably twenty or so.'

'Good. The sooner we act the better, or she might not last the night. We shall put out a general alert, radio stations, television news and so forth. Plus we'll call in as many police as possible from surrounding stations. That's the best that can be done in the circumstances. I suggest we get cracking.'

The law clatters downstairs and out to its paddy wagon, taking with it a sense of purpose and a certain enthusiasm. The nurse asks if she is needed.

'Let's hope this will all blow over and that Vernon might have found her by now. But, yes, I shall need you to help with the search if the search must go ahead. You are going to be very important in this process, Nurse. Very. I'd advise you to change into woollies and waterproofs right away.'

'I'll need Matron to put my juniors back on duty.'

'Leave that to me.'

'Thank you, sir.'

Once she withdraws, the Superintendent pulls up a chair and contemplates the map. Just a map. Yet it has the inscrutability of a warning. Yes, indeed. This is potentially the location of his *disgrace*. There is no time to be lost. By tomorrow the records may be a matter of public knowledge. Police on the loose, the media alerted. The Minister and even the parliament may get in on the act, combing through every last memorandum. So, he has his own tremendous question to address. It begins with the committal and an irregularity the hospital had been utterly unaware of. Dr Parker, depending on how far he'd be determined to push it, could make a lot of trouble. A lot. The unavoidable fact is that the bad luck dogging the one-time Master in Lunacy for most of his professional life looks like striking again. When Lorna Shoddy was delivered to him by ambulance he had accepted her in all good faith, naturally. Though when is good faith ever enough? The issue of *who* had her committed could have been resolved by civilised discussion with this unwanted visitor. If only she herself had chosen some other day to get lost. If only. And there is no way of knowing whether she accidentally wandered away or ... escaped.

He has pulled out the record of her admission. Perfectly in order, so far as it goes. How well it withstands scrutiny will largely depend on whether or not Parker feels tempted to stir up the Australian Medical

Association. Sticky. Yet the Superintendent delays putting a call through to his seniors in Sydney. Why take the plunge unless you're pushed? The point being that Vernon might have picked her up already. Given a bit of time to settle down, all this panic could entirely blow over without trace. A good man, Vernon.

He flips the file open again and examines it. He looks up the details of his first interview with her, when they established that she had no husband or children. His marginal comment of the time reads: *Note: Issue of possible husband further investigated – result negative.* He gives this some thought. He takes his pen and tries it out on a piece of scrap paper to be certain the colour of the ink matches. The same. He now chooses a few words to add: *Asked her to confirm her local doctor's name and whether he put her on medication – incoherent reply.* And then (why not?) he adds lower down: *Our clinical tests confirm local doctor's diagnosis, as per committal papers.* Satisfied, he returns the record of interview to the file where it belongs. Next, he extracts the report of her confinement in the Calm Down room. Also his own subsequent restraining order against her. Finally, he locates the report sheet bearing the date when she was eventually let out of the Calm Down room to be allocated a bed in a dormitory: two of these forms, in Matron's hand, are beyond being tampered with. But he does not replace them. He sits thinking. Eventually arriving at a decision. Having extracted all three documents, he takes them across to the filing

love without hope

cabinet, selects another file at random, notes the name on it, and drops them in.

Half an hour later the van returns.

Three bodies occupy the hospital morgue: two living and one dead. Mark, a young male nurse, stands staring at the corpse on the slab. An experienced orderly, staring in turn at him, nods encouragement. A bare light globe stares at them all. Between Mark and the dead man the sharp knife poises. Mark is in charge of this knife but the knife is the one in focus. Even as it trembles. The young man wags his head helplessly.

'Poor Tom,' he mumbles.

The cadaver is a thin man of perhaps eighty years, a non-person in whom the sap dried decades ago and from whom all living tissue has already been extracted, surrendered filament by filament, through tedious aeons of not being needed. The strands of his personality have been taken too, often painfully. His hopes have been cauterised and the last corrupting trace of happiness surgically removed. The only remarkable feature left him by life is an enormous uncircumcised and unused penis.

'He's been gone a long time, if you ask me,' the orderly contributes.

'Poor chap, he . . .'

Mark slaps the knife down and covers his mouth to stuff the spew back in, then dashes outside into the young night. The orderly lets nothing show. He contents himself with a critical examination of the dead man. Weird to think you can be acquainted with someone on a daily basis, over so many years, without having the least idea what you would say to them if you met them in any other circumstance. And this could be applied in both directions.

As for Thomas Nestor Hopkinson, throughout his life he has been disallowed any function. But now, at last, he will be a help with the training-in-heartlessness of a young nurse. He is an exhibition of mortality. Dead as the dead can be. And thus he achieves the status of an endowment to the establishment, an opportunity. All by himself he has become an implement for breaking in one of those whose business will be breaking others (those, unlike him, who may still be innocent, at least). He has risen to the dignity of educational tool: a sample in the flesh of flesh, though there is little enough of it on his bones.

Mark returns, not looking too well himself. He apologises to his instructor and, approaching the slab again, forces upon himself a second appraisal of the sunken ribs and stringy shanks, that scrub of chest hair, those jutting brows, waxy skin corroded all over with the blisters of some indexed and unsurprising disease, the stain-hardened hands, empty of familiarity, still not yet letting go some heavy tool they have gripped during a lifetime's labour-rich incarceration.

'It's tough, putting the knife in,' Mark gets assured by the voice of experience. 'You wouldn't think it. But we all feel that. The first time. You just have to wind yourself up. Afterwards you get used to it.'

'I suppose.'

Obediently, he again grips the implement, that simplest of precision weapons. The naked steel engages with the cadaver's belly. Old Tom, when alive, could never have hoped to be the hero of the moment, centre of concentrated seriousness, an object respected for being what he is, endowed with the power to hinder a young man's hand, to set him trembling.

'That there is called the breast-bone. You aim just under it,' the orderly advises helpfully.

The point indents the skin.

Living inside it, one would never imagine how tough human hide is. The give of flesh, even in this soft region, sets unmanageable qualms going again. But Mark knows

love without hope

that a man cannot be twice seen to fail in courage. The puncture must be made, however small: the intrusion into a mystery, not knowing what this first prick may let free. Even expecting blood. The point, climax of ages given over to repeated ruthlessness and the implacable urge to bring all argument to a decisive conclusion, suddenly penetrating.

'Funny to think of it,' the orderly ruminates. 'They'll stick sticks into their own ears, these maddies, though you do your best to protect them from themselves. But when it comes to you having to stick the knife in, it's hard. You're doing good, son.'

The cut is drawn longer, smooth and easy now, to reveal thin peelable flaps of white meat and hinted secrets. Relieved, Mark fills his lungs with evil-smelling valour. He has a job to do, a future to look forward to.

The door opens and Matron peers in.

'You'll both be wanted for the search party.'

Neither of them asks *what* search party.

'Right now, Matron?'

'Yes, please.'

So, the attendants on poor Tom Hopkinson back away from him, obediently retreating. Young Mark wipes the dissection knife and replaces it on the appropriate rack and then hovers outside the door for some hint of when he might expect to come back. And that colourless moment of hesitancy under the porch – seeing Matron take the orderly's arm and disappear with him into a lighted doorway, then waiting for them to return so she can tell him what needs to be done, meanwhile sheltering from a light residual rain, glancing the width of the quadrangle and up at the illuminated clock – that very moment unexpectedly becomes the scene of a surprise because the janitor arrives around the corner... the janitor and Vernon with him. The two of them stagger across the yard from Ward Ten, clumsily managing a wicker pallet. They seem oddly nervous that it might tip over and gladly push past into the light of the morgue burdened by the body they're carrying, a body invested with the dignity of a three-piece suit, one shoe, cufflinks and buttoned-up buttons.

Mark stands aside to allow them through, momentarily troubled in case they might shift his humble corpse and displace it with this grander specimen of their own. He watches through the door. But, once in and discovering the slab occupied, they hoist their usurper (who has no rights within the institution) on to the long table under the window instead. The janitor then excuses himself, leaves Vernon to it, and hurries back out, muttering something about problems in the laundry.

So it is that a new corpse, a gate-crasher, comes to lie alongside Tom Hopkinson and settles in where he has been put, imposingly supine, not at all ruffled, wet, but pre-eminent. His respectable belly, his floppy bow tie, handkerchief peeping from his breast pocket. And this is how he presents himself to the tousled mud-smirched Vernon, who stares at him with hatred and amazement: perplexed that the dead doctor is reduced to normal size,

love without hope

really, and shows no sign of that wallowing enormity of the previous hour.

Worse, Dr Parker, recumbent on his throne, actually commands respect by his normality. These are not the limbs of the disinherited, this is not flesh that ever knew what it is to cringe all day, to be shut away from the light, to skulk around shamed by the malformed mind it houses, the damaged spirit. Though, as a corpse, Dr Parker has no further use for that superhuman weight and obstinacy he recently called on, he takes upon himself the breathtaking dignity of the common lot. Composed, in his dead state (and even a touch sanctimonious), he behaves as if nothing happened out there in the fields. That incident with the bull might never have taken place. The delay, the struggle, the nightmarish slowness he forced on Mrs Shoddy's enemies while they floundered down to the van. Even to his final triumphal trick of getting one foot hitched between the struts of the gate, so that he had to be twisted sideways and his knee bent to extricate it, even to his sock snagging on a hook of wire, as an added insult to those who had no intention of rescuing him but who could not refuse the duty of bringing him back with them. Quite apart from which, they knew that once they disturbed the body and moved it from where it fell, they had tampered with it. The tampering was what obliged them to see the job through.

Even now, Vernon marvels at himself, brushing some grass off his elbow while dismissing young Mark

Whatsiname and telling him brusquely to get about his business. Why not leave the dead doctor out there in the paddock where they found him? They could have returned for him later. That janitor! Already Vernon has begun to expunge from the record his own fear of the bull. What's more, as he reasons against this accusation, there was nothing to suggest Lorna Shoddy would go barging on ahead – let alone arrive at the road so much before them. Just why he hadn't removed the BMW's keys from the ignition still baffles him and all he can say is that they weren't his to touch and everyone makes mistakes.

Alone now, he stares at Dr Parker's composedly inert body – far more peaceful than while he was being loaded into the van, persisting in his ungovernable mutiny – a country dignitary. He now presents himself as corpulent, though not exceptionally so. The assorted lumps and falling-away bits (thanks to the gin) are all respectably assembled, endowing him with the disillusioned air of a judge.

Vernon's ruminations, doomed to interruption, are encroached on by more new arrivals: the police come barging in to look the corpse over. So, of course, he makes way, his smile an obstacle and his voice on fire, rescuing his rank by informing them that the Superintendent will send someone to make an inventory of the dead man's valuables, because this is the hospital's responsibility. The morgue is suddenly little better than a meeting place. No sooner has an all-too-capable police-

love without hope

woman introduced herself and remarked that there doesn't seem to be the least sign of anything out of order than the independent medical man they have summoned – arriving from town to issue a death certificate – takes over. So then the rest of them, Vernon included, find themselves back outside, under a clearing night sky and crunching across the gravel to the staff canteen.

Once again, there are just three men in the morgue. But now the dead outnumber the living, where only the one – with his riven tummy – shows any sign of foul play. Archibald Parker's body, having plainly died of that most respectable among diseases, heart failure, now finding itself undressed and looked over, willingly yields the appropriate symptoms to a colleague who can evidently be trusted. Thus Tom Hopkinson, the madman, comes to be sidelined even in the asylum where he belonged for more than half a century and the two doctors (both outsiders) communicate in silence: one surrendering his privacy in the interests of science, the other noting them in all their banality – probably an alcoholic, somewhat obese, unhealthy skin, one malfunctioning knee, some sign of spleen, perhaps mild bladder trouble and an unremarkable bruising just above the right elbow. The main find, an old scar, is a bullet wound in the thigh: undoubtedly the original cause of the lameness. This was a man the right age to have fought in the war and been shot, possibly having displayed gallantry in action. But that's mere speculation. Even so, the corpse begins encouraging it, allowing some hinted expression to show, some confidential intimation of his arrested affronted unreadiness. Yes, Dr Parker has things unresolved. The examiner gently handles his aged arms – lifting, observing, lightly pinching the flesh for what this will tell, taking a look at the tongue and pushing back the lid from a single and terrible one-way eye, laying a hand on his heart, palpating his belly. All this with courteous insistence on a protocol his senior colleague, his late colleague, would appreciate. And, indeed, the corpse cooperatively makes himself accessible, never for a moment confusing such observations with the previous impertinence of amateurs, this being the proper procedure and conducted, as it should be, with dispassionate scrupulousness.

The quiet contains them.

And thus it remains until a functionary from the Superintendent's office lets herself in, explaining simply that she has been empowered. They both resent the intrusion as she begins sorting through the contents of the dead doctor's pockets – even slipping banknotes and credit cards from his wallet, unfolding and scanning scraps of paper, trying out his pen, shaking his watch and extracting his reading glasses from their case to peer through them as if she herself might now be able to see into the mysteries of disease and hypochondria. As she discards each item she places it in one of the wooden trays usually reserved for the property of inmates, property they must resign themselves to never seeing again.

love without hope

Well, the doctor's corpse has been just so resigned long before this. That morning, when he showered and dressed shortly before dawn, making swift choices of what to wear, what to carry, what might be needed in his pockets, he already rehearsed the loss of these things. And he drove out in the still-dark yet shadowy two-dimensionality of silhouettes layered against a paling sky – steering his car into a doomed day – the breaking light already curtained over, though it had barely strengthened enough to see by, with leaden cloudbanks impending above the western horizon, an imperceptibly rising mass of cloud heavier than earth, sandwiching such light as there was, rolling it out till it was paper-thin. And it was into this paper-thin residue that he headed knowingly. All these things the corpse acknowledged and embodied, the hopes and tensions, communicating them to be added to the common store of facts, not neglecting to add his wisdom of acceptance – and being understood by those searching fingers.

'No call for an autopsy here,' the visiting doctor says aloud for the benefit of the office person, who does not matter.

And, even at that moment, he turns his attention to where a pauper's corpse lies on the slab making a show of flesh crudely gashed almost as far down as the *mons pubis*, the stomach laid open in its lurid viscosity, a purple sheen on the blood, the dead sectioned meat, fatless and unhealthy. Minutes tick by while he brings his professional disapproval to bear on this wound, on the clumsy choice of incision, the botched job, on the old-fashioned morgue itself, on his own presence as an intruder into secrets and shame. Shame clogging the air. Grief and pain standing guard at the door. He finds himself thinking that such asylums are defined by the people in them, hapless people, making everyday entrances and exits, shuffling about their wounded routines, bonded to the liberty of digging soil or the liberty of a chance to ease their weary limbs out flat in bed at night, the liberty of swallowing food they need neither catch nor cook, the liberty of compliance with house rules, the liberty of subservience, of humiliation in a life of being looked after and cared for among others of like kind – guarded by the state, protected by orderliness and policy – the hospital a fortress against the chaos they came from, the chaos of unlimited years of never fitting in and never even being recognised as the repositories of their obsessions.

News of the stolen BMW has changed everything. The police, having been notified by the hospital, put word out over the network. Patrols are closing all the main routes out of the area. It is now plain that the miscreant has not just wandered, nor is she lost by accident. She is an escapee. This puts a whole new aspect on the search, already reclassified as a *manhunt*. An official bulletin reports in (and with) confidence that she will soon be caught. Meanwhile, Vernon, sent back to his quarters by the Superintendent for a suggested half an hour's relaxation and a shower, need concern himself no further with the dead doctor.

He accepts the opportunity to unwind.

'Did I,' Vernon reassesses the order incredulously, 'appear stressed, then?'

Yes, while telling the tale of that doctor's interference and Lorna Shoddy's escape he had, indeed, perhaps, grown quite strident. Not a good look. Well, because he prides himself on his pride. He deserves his high reputation and knows it. How else could he continue delivering decisive and reliable service? 'Beyond question my decisiveness – and pretty often at that – has benefited this institution. Plenty of proof on a daily basis.'

Vernon shuts his door. This is his haven, this disused dairy, somewhat negligently converted to accommodation. He doesn't mind the rough and ready job, as a trade-off for having more space than could be expected in the staff quarters. The main luxury being his own bathroom. At least, these days, he need never queue up. Forget the raw concrete floor. Not important. He has fixed a long mirror to the back of the door. Now, every time he sits on the toilet he confronts his double – not unpleasantly. His functions are really quite interesting, his body an inexhaustibly changeable fascination when properly observed. Even to his face going red and his neck swelling with strain.

Something's nagging him, worrying at the heels of his patience? 'Well, I don't like to have necessity force itself in my face. That would be a general way of putting it.'

love without hope

'Whenever an urgent situation arises,' his commentating alter-ego puts in, 'you can't help taking it personally.' 'Such is the cross I bear.' Like this Shoddy business, for instance. Dr Parker's interference was plainly aimed at undermining him. But he accepted the challenge and took swift action. Naturally. Habit dies hard. The fact that this swift action was thwarted by the doctor's accidental good luck in choosing which road to follow was no part of the equation, having nothing to do with it. The one compensation was that the old man had brought the ultimate punishment on himself. 'No one wished him dead, far from it.' 'But out of the way?' 'Maybe, yes. If he had not meddled, that's to say, well, in a matter which was none of his business, he would still be alive, alive and kicking to tell the tale.'

Vernon takes satisfaction in these frank heart-searchings during his private moments because he looks so good. For much the same reason he frequently strips off his shirt as a prelude to shitting. 'The rules I impose in this institution are just and fair. I don't lose my temper.' 'Really?' 'Well, seldom. And I never strike anyone. Others will, other staff *can*, rely on my interest, my impartiality whenever they approach me, well, for advice, or to resolve some conflict.' The only real difference between them and the patients being the stratum they belong in. Layers of the same society. Some fortunate, others less so. 'Some insane,' (he entertains himself with a relaxing witticism), 'others more so.'

He strains to gratify his bowels. Noticing a touch of

soreness about the eyes. Not good. But also noticing swelling shoulders a wrestler would be proud of. 'Brute!' he murmurs indulgently. And then doubts he ever said it. 'But if they oppose me,' he pursues the heart of the matter, 'I'll fuck them. I'll fuck them good and proper. Sure. I'll tighten the rules. I'll stop their cricket, if it's the men. I'll do away with gossip hour for the rest.' Finishing, he doesn't wipe himself because he likes the full sensation of cleanliness. He prefers to step straight under the shower and sluice it away, watching the diluted shit wash down his legs (those hero's legs!) and away, soap slicking him smoother than oil – his body of a Roman gladiator, as he thinks of it – sheathed in metallic brilliance.

Well, there will be more to be done tonight, for certain.

'The system needs me.' 'Exactly, who else can turn his hand to anything at a moment's notice?' Vernon's grasp of the universal is an important element in his pride. He has read a lot in magazines and the newspapers, he keeps himself informed on everything from science to the stock exchange. He can't be faulted. He identifies with others because he accepts that everyone is, more or less, like himself. There's no mystery about a runaway like Lorna Shoddy, he can unerringly predict what she will do and why, because he only need look into himself to find the answer. 'She set out to escape because she thought she could outsmart the system. She has nowhere to *go*, after all. It couldn't be that.' So, she will be found, even without a conspicuous black BMW to give her away. Time will tell. And, though he admits to a sneaky admiring surprise for the fact that she can drive, he accepts this as a further measure of his task. She has become worth his notice again. He had forgotten her since the days when she opposed him on the issue of her insanity, especially that time when she presumed to put her case to the Superintendent in his last days as Master in Lunacy. Since then, while she had needed to be taught her place in the Calm Down room, she qualified only for compassion. And during the interim, Vernon passed her over into the care of the female staff as simply one among many.

He flips the taps off and steps in front of the mirror to watch his image dry itself in the usual orderly fashion, beginning with scrubbing at his wet hair, then the diagonal towel across his back and so on, right down to his toes. Next, he inspects his dryness for approval before reaching for underpants. Contrary to the Super's opinion, he does not need to lie down. Fully refreshed, he will spend a quiet quarter of an hour with his notebook, chancing to open it at *As such, the notion of divinity becomes symbolic of human perfection, an escape from man's often painful limitations.* He hovers over possible improvements, then reviews a new work-party schedule he has been drawing up, rounding it all off with a brief excursion into the encyclopaedia to pursue those tantalising questions: how did Judas die and who was Pontius Pilate?

Anyhow, now she is off his premises, the Shoddy episode is properly an issue for the police... till she is returned.

Once, during the night, Mrs Shoddy wakes to watch two patrol cars cruise along a road on the other side of the valley in which she is parked, perhaps three kilometres away, red and blue lights twinkling as they pass along – headed, roughly speaking, west. Next thing, they are gone: 11.35 by the clock on the dash. She can afford a few more hours' rest. She sets her body-alarm to wake her at three, using that old technique of her father's, thumping her head on the cushioned seat three times. For a horrible moment this thumping calls up some recent memory she has repressed. And demons chase her down a deep hole. But, at the last minute, she escapes into paradise.

1.07 am. The Superintendent, slumped at his desk – head cushioned on folded arms – wakes from a nightmare in which he is back as the Master in Lunacy again and someone's out to get him, some person, some man with the implacable will to murder him piloting a glider of all things, the sleek gull's-egg nose of a glider, fixed wings scything his way. All he can see of his murderer is a terrorist's helmet visible in the approaching cockpit, goggles gazing through the perspex, focused on him – this glider, he somehow knows, has been forty-one seconds out of control, forty-one seconds on its deadly trajectory, being steered straight for his head by a suicidal maniac, the skimming silence, the rigid slicing of dawn air (for it is already dawn in the dream) – so some fanatic he has never met is willing to crash for the sake of killing him.

Two police cars growl along the street outside. He shakes off the panic of helplessness, gets up and stretches, fills the electric jug to make some tea, and returns to his real worries.

3 am on the dot. Mrs Shoddy is up and about. She finishes off the cashews, takes a swig of gin for good luck and starts the car. Good heavens, the motor is so quiet she hardly knows whether it's idling or not, till, once in gear, she finds herself scooped into the night all too powerfully. She snaps on the headlights. She knows where she is.

Things have got so bad for Gail that even while on her way to visit her oldies she appears (to her own mind) a tiny figure lost in a vast landscape of pain – practically *biblical* – her fair freckled skin scorched by the sun and buffeted by wind as she skirts the rim of some stony wilderness. She is filled with fatalistic acceptance of this state of affairs, that a whole desert should expose her, offering no shelter, no succour, no chatty company, no friend to help her on her way, no stranger chancing by to guide her, plus no end in sight. The road appears strange and composed of strangely vivid details sharply picked out by the morning light and long morning shadows. She understands the forty days and forty nights in the desert, scales falling from eyes and the dead in their winding-sheets rising from the grave. Her foot decides for itself when the accelerator is needed and the Ford, on automatic pilot, anticipates each curve, pre-set alert systems guiding it safely around the tricky bits. So she rockets along, overshooting her destination, and continues on toward a house she had thought she would not dare approach . . . not ever again.

Gail knows she must hurry, having passed her last legitimate stopping off place as a community service helper, the last contact authorised by her authorising husband. This is a risk. From here on – if she's caught – her intention will be obvious. And doubtless punishable. But she won't be stopped because sinners (and this is from the Bible, too) are only granted peace of mind by admitting guilt. She will take responsibility. She will stand on that very spot again to make sense of what happened. She has to face her crime. She has something tremendous to confess. Speeding ahead of a vortex of dust and popping stones, she spins in at the open gate, belatedly applying the brakes. The Ford shudders before rolling quietly up the slope (Russell bought her this old rattletrap and she wonders if she thanked him enough for it) and coming to a complete stop.

She gets out.

Leaving the car door open, maybe as a gesture suggesting she won't trespass more than a minute, Gail

love without hope

Savage sets off to walk the rest of the way, her electrified copperwire hair on the alert. That hair. Her father always joked about her face being rusty. Well, now she can feel it, she's so nervous and ashamed. She detours through Mrs Shoddy's orchard of neglected fruit trees, shoes crunching among thistles, till the vista glides into view: a broad prospect of paddocks undulating down to wind-sculpted dunes and the sea. Big old eucalypts stand dotted about the slope, each rooted in a pot of shadow. 'It's a garden!' she murmurs. Yes, Eden. She had not perceived this that day when she and Rita had hurried along the path – in good faith, because when does evil ever show its true face? – all too intent on bearing gifts of food – how very unsuspicious, how terrible a simplicity – but now, as she crosses the back yard to the kitchen door, the whole place strikes her as fixed and peaceful.

Yet (she hesitates) something, some particular thing has shifted or perhaps *tilted*. What? Alert, disquieted, she scans the scene for a clue. Flies spiral above little mounds of manure scattered about the home paddock. She feels some power around her without knowing how to make sense of the feeling. Merging cloudshadows glide sinuously over grassy clefts and bulges. And the heat of the day dries up the last residue of rain. The dam down below the house is rimed with white light, like a vagrant chunk of polar ice. The whole sky races her way, having gathered a silky texture from centuries spent out at sea, and leaves her short of breath. She tries to see what it is that is eluding her. Still the cloudshadows glide. Still the white light rimes the dam. The country itself cups and holds out the answer for her. Just at the moment when she is on the brink of understanding, a play of two wagtails flirting on the fence diverts her. Yet she glimpses some strange magic happening beyond them, the sea props itself on edge as a flat plate of opaque glass, dunes melt away to mercury and scattered moon rocks stand out against the green of earth as if recently dropped from outer space.

She gives it up. This frustrating sense of some lack. She has painful memories to brave. First things first. So, she turns aside to face the house . . . and then, then (released from fact) she sees it. An emptiness. Just that. Gail spins back to check. The horses have gone. The paddocks are uninhabited and the grass rampant. What struck her a moment ago as ravishingly peaceful begins to take on an ominous clarity. The scaly susurrus of dust snaking across the earth, leaf jostling leaf, the uninterrupted depletion. She has no words for this. Struck dumb, she imagines what it must be like for that poor old biddy, shut away up there in the loony bin, to grieve over the loss of such a home. Her scalp crimps and her shoes begin sinking. She feels like a child whose grandmother draws breath ready to tell a fairytale filled with foreboding.

The kitchen door stands open.

Gail has more to learn. And she knows it. The fairytale lures her into the kitchen, where she never actually set foot on that last occasion. The fairytale assures her she can and, emboldened by the creatures of the field scattering at her approach, she does. The fairytale tells of food scraps and filth being turned over to the nation of rats that arrived, prevailed and ruled till their empire fell and they left the scourings to insects and lizards, even birds flying in to nest among the rafters. A silken breeze wraps itself around her. She crosses the kitchen, avoiding mounds of garbage, to venture upon some unexplored horror, in along a passageway where she has no right. Things give underfoot, tiny squelchings and crumblings, the whole place rank with absence. And, just as the fairytale includes a secret chamber, so a bedroom door stands open and ready for her, revealing – as a single blow pierces her heart – Mrs Shoddy.

Gail gazes at her in terror.

It is. It is Mrs Shoddy, under some blankets, drowsy and only just waking up, her little grey head with its hair starting out, her exhausted eyes and one tiny hand, unmistakably hers, gripping the bedclothes, its bones knotted together with blue string. An apparition. Their eyes meet.

'Don't tie me down!' the old lady shouts in a sudden, inconsolable voice.

Promptly, tears spill out over Gail's cheeks. Helpless to control them, she leans in at the doorway. Dread gripping her heart. Dread and shame. Roof-iron clicks in the gathering heat. Cockroaches work at something on a plate.

'I'm so happy to see you,' Gail whispers. 'I came to say sorry. Though I never expected to find you here. We didn't mean to intrude, Mrs Shoddy. We thought we were helping. You can't blame Rita, it wasn't her fault.'

'Why did they hurt me?'

Time gathers between them.

'Did they?'

Mrs Shoddy can hardly understand what is said to her. Yet she shudders at the enormity – as the planets are fixed at appointed distances in the sky, so seem the nails in her brain – the cosmic silence stifling her.

'I've known Rita a long time,' she whispers. 'We never got on.'

This is enough. She struggles to draw torn fragments around her for comfort. And sinks back into the protective oblivion of sleep. Gail, staying to watch over her, suddenly and surprisingly calls to mind her own grief that, at forty-four and never having had children, she lives without anyone she can care for. Well, here is her chance. She has made her confession. Life rewards her with a second chance. For so long lost in the maze of trivia – television soapies, women's magazines, celebrity gossip, the meretricious bric-à-brac of kitchen gadgets and cosmetics, liposuction, Tupperware and wives' morning teas – she has been hungering for this. Already she knows she will stay. The plan leaps to mind fully formed. She will stay in this house if she is allowed. At least while Mrs Shoddy lives.

'The government has taken your property,' she confesses to the sleeping woman. 'That was the council's doing. It all took months. They put it up for sale to

love without hope

pay the arrears. And my husband sold it for them.'

And Mrs Shoddy hears her in her dream of the asylum. But she cannot prove who she is, because they've withheld her driver's licence, flipping it into a wooden tray with her precious remnants of independence: her Land Rover keys, her purse, the dried-out lipstick she might one day apply again as she used to, the strip of aspirins, the amethyst that fell out of its setting and which she always meant to have fixed back in the claws of the engagement ring Martin gave her. Tissues, a couple of hairpins and a stub of pencil.

Gail sits on the edge of the bed and takes that tiny cold hand to warm it between her own, feeling the progress of the nightmare even as it subsides.

So, Mrs Shoddy dreams of her mother. Her mother has picked her up and swept her to her bosom. Her mother has spoken her name and patted her back. Her mother has brought her a steaming cup of hot milk with the wrinkling milk-skin that clings to her lip like a bridal veil when she drinks. The milk has been sweetened. And now she will sleep.

'But they can't do this to you, can they?' Gail says. 'You have the education to stop them.'

Little Lorna, being rocked in a cradle, regurgitates the milk. Her mother will clean up any misunderstanding with the Master in Lunacy. She is about to speak to the Master when she is told that he is urgently needed in Ward Ten because some old man is dying there, but she can wait if she pleases and put her case to him when he returns, though she should be aware that once the great man touches the head of someone dying it takes days for him to recover his equilibrium – so exhausting is his sympathy – therefore anyone wishing to present a petition is better advised to wait a while and come again when the doomed patient is fully dead and buried. She finds herself tumbling down a staircase with her pleas unheard, the injustices she suffers unaddressed, bruised and wending her way back to the dormitory, where Julie gives her the signal to watch out and she feels the swoop of air as a distraught Nurse Felicity rushes up to ask where she has been and how she could bring herself to betray her friends on the staff by taking her complaint above their heads. She has no answer for this.

'I have to go now,' Gail explains. 'But, if you'll let me, I shall bring you some food tomorrow. Not the cooking I do for the old folk. I'll bring special things like I cook for Russell. And fresh milk and tea. And then we'll get your stove going and we can be snug.'

Mrs Shoddy remembers Dr Parker arriving in his suit and the massive hunching stubbornness of him, the awkward feet, the thick neck and small eyes. But also his kindness and the etchings of sorrow.

'If you see Archie,' she mumbles in the voice of one absent, 'you'll thank him for me, won't you?'

Aware of her hand being surrendered back into her own keeping, she slips it in under the covers. She will sleep now. She will look for her horses in the morning.

'I'll be back,' says Gail.

love without hope

Then she steps out into the dazzle of the day, the empty fields and the overfull sky. Her heart sings with grief and gladness. Next time she must find some way of concealing her car – because she will return – so she peeps into the old tractor shed to check that out, thinking it might be a good place. To her astonishment she finds Dr Parker's BMW there. Unmistakably Dr Parker's. This presents a bit of a puzzle. What can it mean if the doctor is here? Might he be somewhere in the house? Watching? Watching over Mrs Shoddy? And he's the only Archie she knows of, though she'd never dare be so casual with him. This throws some doubt on her plan to come back. She supposes *she* is the one without rights when it comes to the point. Humbly, she drags the big door shut again and makes her way down the track, deep in thought, scarcely aware of a vehicle passing along the road beyond the gate, let alone suspecting she has been spotted... or that this may be why the driver accelerates in a swirling camouflage of grit, rushing toward town to be sure of getting there first.

The door to the Ford stands open. And, for just a moment, this seems puzzling.

Mrs Shoddy, explaining her escape to Martin, deals with his questions one at a time.

'Well, darling, I set off again while it was still dark. Oh, that is such a comfortable car. Of course, it was only a matter of time before I reached a familiar road. Considering all those years we floated our horses up to shows, it only stands to reason . . .'

Martin is laughing and his laughter is a tonic. Yes, she gets it: the word *reason*. And she wriggles snugly under the blankets, her shivering already forgotten in a moment of merriment.

love without hope

'It's a good thing we can laugh,' he ruminates, 'because things have gone bad for me. The Croatian government is caving under pressure. It looks as if I might lose all this...'

She sees it, then, the island glowing with sunlight, the old stone quay, the Roman galley-house, now paved and used as a market because the sea has sunk and the shoreline is broader, the lovely hillside of jumbled houses, the little cathedral with its Venetian campanile, open squares, the absence of traffic and that languorous pleasing of the senses so typical of the Adriatic. And she sees what its loss might mean.

'Poor Martin,' she murmurs.

'Poor me,' he agrees. 'Bad egg that I am.'

They laugh together, though she is shaking most dreadfully.

'But you showed them, Martin. You called their bluff.'

'And took their money.'

They lapse into their separate thoughts.

'I've no intention of giving in or going down, Lorna,' he declares. 'I shall find a way out.'

'You do that.'

'I received your letter, thank you. And I shall come for you.'

'I always believed, I always believed you would.'

'Keep your eye on the news, old girl.'

Oh yes, she'll keep her eye on the news all right. Contentment flows to the deadened tips of Mrs Shoddy's fingers. The news. Yes. After a few minutes he takes up the tale again.

'The point is that I have a conscience. When I went adventuring I was a genuine traveller, never a tourist . . .'

'Meanwhile collecting information, though, and passing it on?'

'That too, admittedly.'

'Who to?'

'Never you mind, my dear.'

'I wish you hadn't.'

'It can be fun being the bad guy, though.'

'Till they catch up with you. Or till you're needed at home.'

'But don't envy me. You're better off with your horses. They're real.'

'They waited for me, you know.'

'Life on this island is no life at all. Not for a red-blooded woman, anyway: a hairdresser in residence, maids for the work, a cook to make every decision about food tiresome, two gardeners to keep the garden a picture, a secretary for dealing with the flood of pleas from various charities – every day brings more of them – people needing charity don't care how you make your money. Spying or Hollywood, it's all one to them. You live in seclusion because that's what wealth drives you to. You talk to only a very few chosen friends, and still you can't tell whether they're real friends or not. There's no way of knowing if they give a damn about you. You grow soft (even me, though I've installed a gym in the

love without hope

house), you plunge into your private pool, you swim a few laps, give up for no good reason and get out when you feel like it. Every day the same. The day itself has no markers, no imperatives, no shape apart from the rising and going down of the sun.'

He gives her a moment to think about this.

'My difficulty is getting out,' he explains, 'because everyone knows me.'

'But you're a *spy*. You can arrange it.'

'I can't leave the island. The international police would have me in jail quicker than the warrant could be signed. They've all read my books. Or the first book, at least. As for the island itself? Well, let me tell you about the life I lead. I live behind closed shutters. Let's say I decide to go for a walk along the waterfront one day, the most perfectly picturesque port anyone could ever imagine, just to stretch my legs and soak up a bit of local atmosphere, perhaps to watch some fishermen unload their day's catch, then wander across to the covered market and buy a few fresh figs, flop on a rickety chair at a rickety little table in the sun and sip a Pernod – all very well – I can do it, sure, but I'd better be ready for everybody (and by everybody I mean every child and its dog) to identify me. The local crooks at their restaurant doors raise their Panama hats and give me a wicked wink. Tourists crane their necks. Twenty Japanese ladies in sun visors are sure to be aiming their lenses at me already, and next thing it's a battery of home video cameras, some blatant, others surreptitious, capturing my slightest response with auto-focus precision. And every one of these sleuths has at the back of his or her mind the possibility of catching me off-guard, getting a shot of me into which they hope to read some new scandal that they can sell to the world's press. I am their golden moment, sheltering behind my sunglasses. A nightmare.'

'Sounds lovely,' she whispers dreamily. 'Figs, you say? Go on.'

The sale complete, contracts exchanged and the money, more than he had ever got for any other property, safely in his bank (eighty-five percent of it to be paid out to the Public Trustee, yes, but a very tidy sum to be kept), Russell says nothing of this to Gail when she arrives home. But he does notice she seems oddly flushed, which doesn't suit her complexion. He makes up his mind. No backing down. She hasn't spoken a word to him since the buyer came to the house. Once, they did confront each other in the middle of the night, she coming out of the bathroom when he was going in.

'So, there you are, then,' he'd said, 'unless I'm hallucinating!' And he'd regretted the attempt at a jest because her eyes went stony and she turned side-on to avoid physical contact.

Each evening he comes home to find his dinner in the oven – and Gail at that moment locking herself in the spare bedroom. Each morning he gets up to the smell of breakfast laid out on the table. All day she goes bush in her old car, he never has any idea where. In short, this is a stand-off and it cannot be tolerated. He must defend his pride. What drives him wild is that the business is a success, at last, which any normal wife would be grateful for. Mother Gibbons is on his side, too. The other day the old duck stuck her head over the garden fence to ask: How's business, Russ? She'd looked pretty smug herself. And why not (God knows she did little enough for the pay-out she scored) and she'd wished him luck. Luck with what?

The only plan he has in mind is something no one can know. And he will go through with it. The decision is made. He arrives home, slamming the front door, to be greeted by sounds of activity from the kitchen. So, she's running a bit behind time this evening? He smells dinner cooking. Best to leave her to her own devices. Meanwhile, occupying himself with some contract work in the livingroom, he sticks a disc on the record player. There's nothing like rock'n'roll when you're stewing with anger. Ten minutes later, he hears a bedroom door click shut and a key turning in the lock. He stops the disc. The

love without hope

house falls quiet. Time for food. He shuffles out and sits down to a steak cooked exactly as he likes it, chips – she's a dab hand at chips – and peas. Just the thing. He tucks in. Good humour begins creeping up on him.

Gail, behind her locked door, chews her own hateful meal. Having once washed it down with a cup of tea, she gets busy (her overnight bag was safely stowed in the boot of the car hours ago, together with spare shoes, toiletries and groceries) packing a box with flour, lard, mince, onions – the things she whisked out of the kitchen at the last moment – ingredients for a couple of large meat pies. Evidently, she cannot bake the pies at home. He'd know. He may even put her on the spot, trying to guess who they're for. She can cook them at the CWA, no problem. She checks her list. She has her escape organised. Before dawn she will put out his breakfast of cold-cuts and set off on foot for the CWA. It's not far. This way she won't risk waking Russell with the car starting up. Once there, she'll have a couple of hours clear. She can pop some nice pies in the oven. Russell will have left to open up the snack bar. So, she can walk home. She needn't even go into the house. Everything she needs is in the Ford. Bob's your uncle, she'll drive back to the CWA by eight, pick up the cooked pies and be gone. For good. By the time Sally arrives at ten (because Sally's the one rostered to clean the hall ready for the monthly meeting) she herself will be well on the road to Mrs Shoddy's place and freedom.

Propped on a walking stick of torchlight, Nurse Felicity advances through the ward. The patients are restless. Beds squeak and shudder as she passes. Mutterings and snuffles come from all round, betrayals of the female animal. The light grovels along coir runners. This is routine. Except for the nurse's own heart. Distressed, she finds that she's breathing in the very same misery and bitterness they breathe out. Infected with their yearnings. She feels their simple imprisoned hopes and humiliating appetites. The whole dim space is blurred by Felicity's tears. Her throat is so clogged she must take

love without hope

hold of it with her free hand. And, at this moment, she comes upon a folded nightie at the foot of the only empty bed in the whole place. The tremendous question, holding her rigid and refusing to let her go is: what if Lorna Shoddy was never insane?

She prays an unbidden prayer that frightens her. *Dear God, don't let us... just in case... don't let us... capture her again.*

Shit! Russell Savage thinks. It's dawn already. Another minute or so and I will be too late. Fool! Fool! For a smart guy, soon to move back to the city, this is not so smart. He struggles into his pants and carries two suitcases of personal things out to the Toyota to stow in the boot.

Already a couple of farm workers drive past on a tractor dragging a harrow, grinning at each other, like the yokels they are, with the ingrained stupidity of a lifetime's repetitive work. Russell has no time for them. All too often he has had to fraternise with their kind,

love without hope

man to man, when the chance came to lure them away from the rut of outdated routine and brain-numbing toil into taking financial decisions, putting the family land on the market for subdivision into housing blocks. They haven't seen him. Good. He lurks behind the Toyota while their machinery, like a working model of their collective brain, clatters and jounces past in the gloom with infuriating slowness. Being seen would spell disaster. He plays safe and waits till they have fully rounded the corner. He had intended to act before such fellows were up, let alone on their way to work. Well, they're gone, so these particular idiots won't be the ones to stop him.

Still with bare feet, Russell hobbles back for his shoes. But, no – cancel that thought – barefoot and tousled is certainly better. He should get on with it, meanwhile making no noise. Whatever happens ... whatever happens, Gail must not be disturbed. That's the main thing. Shirtless, he gets busy under the spare bedroom window. Determined not to lose his nerve. Still plenty to be done. Then he crosses the yard, completely unaware that he may have been observed.

Rita Gibbons's migraine has propped her up in bed, as on countless other mornings, and clasped her hands across her stupendous bosom. At the first spill of dawn the cloud of pixels, to which her sight is atomised by pain, assembles itself as a novel tableau: Russell Savage, up already, ducks behind his car, apparently keeping watch on the road (which she cannot see). Hiding? She is further intrigued by his antics as he re-emerges once the coast, so it seems, is clear. Rita, martyr to migraines and an artist at expressing every excruciating detail of her sufferings to whoever has an interest – many a time others have learned what it's like from her, besides benefiting from her wisdom as an expert in comparative analgesics – gets the picture clearer. Despite her lace curtain shifting about in the breeze, its wafted folds hazily obscuring the scene (out of reach, just when she'd like to hook the wretched thing back and give herself a clear view), she makes out plenty enough to keep her alert.

With a show of reasonableness she asks her husband's sleeping form what, in the name of all that's wonderful, the Savage creature could be doing loading his four-wheel drive at such an hour? She takes note that Gail's old Ford is parked in its usual place. But no sign of *her*. The migraine mellowing with use, she witnesses more antics as Russell hastens around on tender feet, carrying a fuel can, would you believe? The square can. The one he keeps in the garage for the lawnmower (there is very little she misses where her neighbours are concerned). One of the beauties of life in a country town is that you *do* get to know. And you get known. This is what knits a community together. She has the drill by heart, every item of every routine.

One more irregularity catches her eye: the Savages' dog is off the chain. Yes. And there goes Russell, chasing

love without hope

it away from the kitchen door. Stupid little pug, she always did despise the breed. When she was young she had mastiffs. This was because her father had established a tradition, besides setting other standards for the entire district. The pixelated pug tries to scramble back into its kennel. Rita cannot quite see from this angle, but she hears a couple of yaps. Next thing, Russell returns, having scooped it up, shushing it with kisses. Still with bare feet. She notes this disapprovingly (because there's no surer way to catch a chill than going barefoot), carrying the petrol can in the other hand. He puts the dog in the car but he shuts the door so cautiously it's not latched. He loves that little rat of a thing. And now he returns the can to the garage.

Out again, his behaviour gets odder and odder. What's he looking at? She has him clearly in the frame, shifting from one foot to the other. Evidently expectant. Watching something ... but what? Apart from his house itself? She cranes further to see. No good. He appears jumpy as all get-out. 'Just look at that,' she recommends to her husband's turned back. And Arthur lets out a bit of a snore. Sharply, Russell swings round to stare her way. But, of course, with daylight only just breaking and so little of it, there's no way anybody could see in. Not to mention her lace. Something else peculiar happens ... with lights going on in there. Now that the migraine has loosened its grip she is fully attentive. Weird, flickering lights.

'Arthur! Arthur,' she shrieks, her mountainous flesh

a-tremble with excitement, and whacks at her husband's presented rump. 'Fire!'

At one bound, Mr Gibbons is on his feet, old as he has grown, a bushman born and bred. Already stumbling down the side steps, he hoists his emergency fire hose on one shoulder. Out through the gate and in at theirs. She sees his striped pyjamaed form shove past Russell, making for the nearest water outlet. Good man. But the interruption gets Russell jumping, as if he's been stung, hastily hobbling away on tender feet round the front – why the *front* of the place when he emerged from the back? – not to mention acting more bizarrely than ever, banging at his own door (heavens to Betsy!) and rattling the handle like someone in an episode of *Neighbours* giving an impersonation of a frantic attempt at rousing the household. What household? There's just him and Gail, after all. Besides, Rita always did say they were bringing trouble on their own heads with those deadlocks they'd had fitted. Anyway, she gets the phone snugly nestled in her lap and puts the receiver to her ear. She's on to the brigade without taking her eye off the drama outside.

Flames swiftly establish a hold. How could it happen so fast? She approves as her husband – no less handy at this than when he was young – busies himself with the unhurried routine of clipping his hose to the Savages' garden tap and spinning the spigot. Then, when the first of the water coughs and splutters out, he smashes a French window. As the sparkling jet firms up, having the

love without hope

appearance of a length of rope that's pulling him indoors, he steps through like a hero, disappearing in a welter of black smoke.

Russell hops about on the spot and shouts: Gail something . . . something Gail. Several other neighbours have arrived to help. That Queenslander on the far side is passing a full bucket to her grown son and sending him to charge in with it. Smoke, like a giant shadowy cauliflower, abruptly balloons from the open bathroom window. There's more to this fire than Rita thought. Russell, yelling by now, has all the appearance of whipping himself into a frenzy. He'll suffer a conniption if he keeps that up, she thinks sourly.

The fire truck is turning in at the gate and lads leap off, still woolly with sleep, but eager. She puts names to them – one by one – because this helps clarify her mind and ease the migraine. Indeed, she finds she can get up. She attempts this with care. Yes. And, standing, she reaches for her dressing-gown. The boys will be glad of a pot of tea when the job's done. Plainly that won't be long. They have the place surrounded and all the equipment you could ever want. Her Arthur retraces his steps, emerging backwards, still playing his hose on the blaze. Well, that's a relief. She ties the girdle of her gown.

The smoke changes colour, lightening, and already the men take to marching indoors and out, pretty well at their pleasure. There are plenty of instructions being barked, plus the occasional blurt of laughter. Goodwill all round. Her vision clearing, Rita reaches for the curtain to loop it out of the way. Who cares if she is seen now? She smooths her hair, still cautious how she raises her arms, not to upset her head. In this gesture of amazement she finds herself arrested ... by the sight of Gail. Gail, none other! Gail in the distance, way down the street, fully dressed in her going-out clothes and hurrying this way, a basket on her arm. Looks as if she's been up for hours.

A few more carloads of volunteers draw up and more lads pile out to see what can be done. But the fire is under control. And here comes Gail, panting in through her own garden gate. On top of everything else, the event becomes all the more spellbindingly unpredictable – and this takes the cake – when the husband rushes out of his smoky house, looking totally crazy and distraught, only to run slap-bang into his wife. What Rita Gibbons observes at that moment, which she will never forget, is the change in Russell Savage: his flushed face being suddenly twisted by a look of startled and uncomprehending fury.

At night the spirits gather in attendance. Mrs Shoddy cannot get warm. Yet she knows she has been chosen. And, as all the chosen throughout the ages come to testify, this is an uncomfortable privilege – witness, the two thousand seven hundred of them martyred for the Catholic cause alone – she is especially frightened by Saint Agatha, poor mutilated thing. Agatha, having withstood her breasts being cut off rather than betray her faith, carries them around on a plate. And in a psychiatric hospital it might very well be the sort of occurrence to merely raise an everyday alert among the staff, calling on their routine efficiency at rushing the victim (of whoever's hand, even her own) into the infirmary to be patched up with the minimum fuss.

Oh, she loves this night. Here she has a window for looking through. Darkness is the only thing it has in common with those closed and stuffy nights of dormitory walls. And even the darkness glitters with mysterious luminosity. This is a night she can look deeply into. And she gazes until her rapture becomes delirious.

She asks: 'How shall I recover from the goodness of horses?'

Confused voices babble in Mrs Shoddy's head, spirits out there in the yard among hulks of rusted machinery and piles of old tractor tyres, an upturned bath with the stumpy legs of a slaughtered pig. Spirits among the fruit trees. Blossoms. What's the difference? She believes that a breath of perfume may be a spirit, at the moment when it is taken into your body for the senses to recognise. Her entrails are now wholly eaten out and her flesh clenches round the agony of a trembling sickness, her poor damp throbbing limbs, yet a voice caresses her from time to time with the one elaborated refrain, like a keening.

'This is Gail. Do you know me, Mrs Shoddy? I first came a while back and I'm sorry. Now I am here again, but I'm here for you. It's Gail Savage. Do you remember? You've got a terrible fever, I'm afraid. If you'll let me bolster you up I can feed you some chicken broth. I boiled this just for you. To do you good and warm your cockles. I'll stay with you. And I've baked us a pie for later.'

love without hope

Next, the ghost of Mrs Shoddy finds herself propped on pillows, light-headed while some incandescent fluid maps her gullet all the way down from throat to gut. Is she not a ghost at all? At this elevation – and now that it is daytime – she can look out of the window, over the tragic fateful too-bright earth where for so many years she has made her living from the fertility of her beloved slaves.

And she is definitely not alone.

She gets this freckled young woman in focus. Mrs Shoddy sees her kindly insipid expression, the troubled face of the guilty, and hears her repeated rubric of *Gail Gail* . . . As if I don't already know, she thinks. Belonging to the soil among the horses her father purchased (especially once she brought her own strategies to the breeding program), to live and breathe breeding until the breeding took over as a dream, sustaining her with its incorporeal and illogical mythology, its matching of bloodlines – the theoretical boundaries of a liquid, demarcations of the indivisible – which she understood by divination more than the charts she drew for her father's approval. Her father, who never understood. Now she remembers Martin when he first looked the property over with his lopsided grin and told her she must be a true daughter of the soil not to see for herself that the spirits of the place had hold of her already, not to mention those extra ones he brought along with him from his own family.

She is a museum of the days she has lived, so many days crowding in on her, till days and spirits become all the same and a swirl of wind. She senses them and their disturbance. Herself as a child, in the early morning spaciousness of a little church, the priest's bespectacled face illuminated and framed by whitewashed walls as he prayed for rain, even while she dissented by praying instead for her father to be cured of the drink, or sometimes praying for a lover. And walking home in winter, frost still crusting the ground, even though a carpet of feeble sunshine lay over it in gilded and glorious delicacy. As a young woman she'd still blush when she admitted her thoughts and remembered her devotions and her seeking, her self-seeking, hopes. In time, that liberty she enjoyed with horses grew so inspired no one quite knew whether such powers could be explained. But horse magic, being an ancient craft, the language itself remembers it. She hit her stride and grew confident.

So, when Martin began neglecting her and drifted away into his own regions – despite the fact that she never imagined them to include ambitions of notoriety – she told herself she couldn't recognise him, though plainly she could. She told herself he no longer lived with her. Even when his body penetrated hers, she could say he was somewhere else. Until he was. And the precise moment of his leaving, both in body and spirit, passed without notice.

She had not expected to miss him, yet she did. She missed him with the keening of her flesh. Still does. And now, to her surprise, she finds she can rejoice because it is a reminder and proof of being alive. At last, she cherishes

love without hope

the anguish and fury she felt against her own misjudgement in letting him go, her wilful self-bereavement. For what is independence but a crippling vanity? And there was quite some resentment against her among the farming community of men, who said a woman couldn't run a property by herself – not least because she went on to hurt their self-esteem by doing so. Even their wives showed some resentment. Only Elsie Southwell stuck up for her.

A sign of the times, with her father gone and her husband gone, she had begun thinking about people and how people are: as if she'd not had the leisure for such thoughts before. She put new value on Elsie, on the doctor and the doctor's wife. She took to inviting them all over for whist. She helped mind their dogs and their houses if they went away. Elsie sometimes came along for the drive when Mrs Shoddy took her horses to be shown in other towns.

Her thoughts are interrupted by that persistent voice: 'What would *you* do if your husband tried murdering you?' she finds herself being asked out of the cycle of hours and the rising tide of a fever. 'What if . . . what if he set fire to the house to burn it down with you in it?'

But Lorna of the Calm Down room offers no ready answer, she has never thought of such a thing. A house being a place to be safe in. Mind you, she thinks of it now. She has reason to be grateful that Martin left, as an alternative to growing to hate her. Though he would never have done anything awful or spiteful to harm her. Somehow the questions are a help. She finds she can call on (and wind up) all the grief she has felt and see something in it she never saw before.

The questions keep coming: 'If he did, would you accuse him of attempted murder, like Rita says it was? Because Rita saw the whole thing from her place. Would you take him to court?'

Mrs Shoddy, discovering fresh reserves of strength and tapping into them, cranks herself up to speak.

'My life was ruined by fire, too,' is what she can finally offer, feeling the fire in her blood even now and smelling scorched horsehair, groping around her for some pliers and a way to free her darlings from the prison of their panic. 'That's how I came to be like this.' She holds up her hands as if others might see what she cannot feel: the dead nerve-endings. Her hands tremble uncontrollably.

Gail feels a certain consternation at talking to a person so evidently educated, but overcomes it in the interests of necessity. This is her chance. She has to talk. She has to confide: 'The insurance people say that an electric fault began that fire. Nothing more. The policeman says so, too. They all believe Russell. So what hope is there for the truth?'

'Well, you can take some satisfaction, Gail,' Mrs Shoddy offers brightly and her own words sound so very convincing to her, 'in having survived this misfortune, because that will be what throws your shadow on the ground in front of you when you walk out in the morning.'

love without hope

She has her second wind. She's ready to add something even more helpful, but holds back because she can't be quite certain about the train of what she might mean to say. What's more, her own shadow crashes across the bed among tree shadows, trees so disturbed by wind that a body could go giddy watching them up on the wall beside her (which she can see reflected in the wardrobe mirror), as she witnesses herself, spoon in claw, now able to manage the steaming nourishment she is offered by a woman she once thought of as her enemy.

'Good girl,' says Gail, as if encouraging a child with the offer of a second helping.

'I am a good girl,' Mrs Shoddy agrees, reminded.

Another ladleful of soup steams in the bowl. But, of course, she has no evidence that Martin ever went travelling or wrote a book. It's what she hopes.

Olga Ostrov thinks she has solved the enigma of where Gail fled to. The whole town is abuzz since Russell's wife, having made her wild accusation – that he set light to their house to murder her – ran away from home. When the police declined to arrest him on her say-so, because she wasn't even inside (and the fire damage proved not much worse than the water damage), she just vanished. No one knew where. Till yesterday, when Olga herself caught a glimpse. Gail was standing beside her parked car at Mrs Shoddy's gate, of all places!

So, now she can help Russell, who has gone oddly

quiet about the whole incident. The fury she feels against that woman is a private matter and need concern no one else. She herself is determined not to let it intrude or compromise her professionalism. Her right to some happiness, at last, is her own affair. She comes to a decision.

The issue in question is this: any squatter found camping in an empty house raises legal complications and a potential obstacle to fair trade because forcible eviction can be contested and takes time. Despite the exchange of contracts on the property, Russell cannot feel safe until the deed is safely wrapped up. She would hate him to lose out at the last minute. That would be so unfair. Meanwhile, she is comforted by his assurance that the demolition work has been slated and can begin the moment the men arrive with their machinery. So, the scene is set. And Olga, having brought herself out here, slews in at the gate to park alongside Mrs Shoddy's abandoned Land Rover. She applies the handbrake.

As quietly as possible, because she needs to catch Gail red-handed in order to – well – persuade her to leave, she clicks the car door shut. She smooths her starched uniform. Then looks around. The first thing she finds is Gail's old Ford, hidden at the back of a tumbledown carriage shed. In the interests of thoroughness she seizes the big door to the shed itself and eases it ajar, just to have a squint. And discloses, to her astonishment, Dr Parker's BMW glittering blackly in the striped gloom! Even supposing Gail is planning to spoil the sale as a way of getting back at her husband, what on earth does

Dr Parker have to do with it? That hateful patronising old man who never once referred any of his patients to her and snubbed her in the street the very week she arrived in the district. Well, now she might have something on him. But caution is called for. A doctor – whether or not he's a drunk – constitutes a force to be reckoned with. It's one thing for the missing wife to go sneaking off and holing up in an empty house, but quite another for *him* to hide his car in the shed.

Olga takes a deep breath. She is definitely making progress. The only thing she fears is that the gossips might stumble upon some connection between herself and the sale, or at least the fact that she proposed the sale of the property in the first place. But still, provided she doesn't accidentally encounter the new owner here, she should be all right. And certainly there's no hire car or helicopter to be seen. So far, so good. Okay. Now it's time to tackle the house itself. She can face anything, even Dr Archibald Parker MD. A nurse always has the excuse of being able to pay visits in the interests of others. She steels herself with a reminder of Russell's threat that, if the big deal falls through, he will renege on his special offer to her.

Olga turns her back on the carriage shed. Braced, justified and making ready to bring her calming skills to bear, she steps boldly through the orchard towards the house to present herself at the back door. And. Out of the blue, Gail stands there, confronting her, Gail, all elbows, her spiky hair starting up in a brazen crown, blocking the doorway like a bushranger's moll (as Olga describes the scene later) with a dusty shotgun in her hands.

The miscreant aimed straight at my heart, Olga's police report reads, *putting my life at risk*.

However, that isn't the end of the incident. No. She escapes in terror, blundering away round the corner to make a dash for her car, slams herself in and escapes down the drive ... but just as she is about to swing on to the road the way ahead is blocked by a colossal WIDE LOAD vehicle, vast tyres stitching the dirt, looming right on top of her. With no way round it she throws the car into reverse – expecting a gunshot from Gail to shatter her window at any moment – and, as fast as she dares, backs off to leave the way clear. The driver waves acknowledgement as he veers in at Mrs Shoddy's gate. She waits nervously, still frightened and not wishing to be seen by anyone else. But, at the last moment, the truck stalls and grinds to a halt, unable to fit past the Land Rover. The driver and his mate climb down to confer, scratching their heads. One decides:

'Simplest thing is to slip her into neutral and push the damn thing out of the way, mate.' He then turns to Olga. 'Perhaps you wouldn't mind hopping in and steering it for us, Sister.'

So she comes to sit in Mrs Shoddy's four-wheel drive on Mrs Shoddy's own seat, viewing the landscape framed as her victim saw it for so many years. She grabs at the gear stick and forces it into neutral, then lets out the brake. The whole experience gives her the creeps – the feel of the vinyl under her, the bag of mouldy brown apples on the passenger seat, the gritty rubber floor – as she feels herself being pushed aside by manpower.

The Superintendent, having called in his senior staff for a briefing, offers them coffee and biscuits. The room is so stuffy they suspect he has been at his desk all night: slumped there, doubtless, stewing on the implications of the emergency. They can see it, too, gouged in his cheeks, plastered on his greasy skin and glueing his eyes. He has the light-shy lostness of a criminal just emerging from under some prison portal, a man disoriented by his early release from detention, a man who can keep what he knows to himself, but who must face life out in the weather, wearing his inappropriate clothing of a lost time with the niggling shiftiness of having got away with something. The two doctors attending declare precedence and sit first, then Matron takes her turn.

'I am inviting Felicity and Vernon to join us,' the Superintendent begins and nods toward the open door, through which the named staff emerge (Felicity hesitant and Vernon smirking) to join the conference.

With one finger he pins a scrap of paper to his desk, ready for later.

'I am sure you will be relieved to know,' he gets his decayed voice going, 'that we can now bring the Lorna Shoddy episode to a satisfactory close. As you are aware, the Department was due to commence its investigation today. I have just spoken to the Minister in Sydney.' A flicker of conceit prompts him to clarify this: 'I took the liberty of phoning the Minister at home. And, fortunately, my call came in time to save his departmental officers making a trip here for nothing. The upshot is, I am pleased to say, that he sends his commendation to you all. For the work you do. And the work you have done. This upheaval simply provided us with a test case – as I took the opportunity of pointing out to him – by which we can measure the quality of care and service we deliver. To the community. And especially to the community of the needy.'

One doctor, the Chinese one, crunches his biscuit, at last, and blows on his mug of instant coffee. The Superintendent now takes up the scribbled note, watched, very

love without hope

particularly by Vernon Ross, sitting erect on the edge of his chair, with the satisfied wary unelastic vigilance of the chosen. Felicity, next to him, loyally touches his knee with hers, in a brief gesture void of the least sexual implication. Indeed, she looks drawn and worried.

'A stolen car, as you will recall, was the patient's means of escaping. I am in a position to report that this vehicle has now been located, hidden in a farm shed . . .' he checks the note before him – being visited by a sudden sinking premonition that he might have misread it the first time – snatching at the flimsy thing, discovering he has it upside down and then leaning to peer at it, baffled, and having to bring his eyes into focus, '. . . on Lorna's former property. Frankly, no one had thought of looking there. Action is being taken right this minute. But Lorna Shoddy herself is not a case for the police. She's one of ours. And who knows what state she may be in? Now we know where to look for her we shall bring her straight back here to be cared for.'

Both doctors begin chewing in unison.

'So,' the Superintendent winds it up, 'I am asking Vernon and Felicity to set off to collect her without delay. The ambulance is being brought round.'

Nurse Felicity pictures herself helping to hold the old lady down while Vernon lashes the camisole on. Already she imagines the desperate screaming. But, no, before that can happen, they have a long drive ahead of them, several hours, a drive down the dangerous prevarications of the mountain road. Anything might happen. Would an accident be justified? Herself the perpetrator? Or should she plead – appealing to Vernon's kindly nature – and bring reason to bear? In turmoil she listens miserably as the Superintendent concludes what he has to say.

'We shall soon be able to welcome Lorna home. And an unfortunate chapter can be brought to a close. I don't suppose we shall ever know what got into her, but she would seem to have come to no particular harm. For this we must be grateful. But what a fuss! Well, my friends, that's about it. Any questions?'

Mrs Shoddy thinks she can hear an approaching storm. But as yet it's no more than a rumble, oddly sustained. Lying in bed, she looks out on her home country basking in steady light, fixed with the fixity of ever after. This feels like a saint's day and probably is. Each tree stands in its customary pot of shadow. Upright remains upright. Reflections on the dam lie flat. And down at the sea's edge sculpted dunes expose flanged and sensuous curves to the sun. Grass-hoppers swarm unharmed and unswept from the sky till the not-impeded birds swoop among them for a mid-air harvest. Mrs Shoddy stares with the most intense eye-mindedness she can muster.

'It's nothing,' she decides.

Sunk as she is in a rapture of fevered blood, she is haunted by the strangely peaceful surprise of stroking a bull's black flank. A colossal bull wreathed in mist somewhere down the track. She feels an urgent need to return Archie Parker's walking stick, too. She needs to say goodbye to him and all of a sudden finds herself weeping fierily, unable to shake off the mood. She has debts so great they overwhelm her. But Archie is talking to her. So, how did it happen, Lorna? he asks, shaking his damp shaggy head. And she tries her best to pull herself together. Well, Archie, she replies, that's all water under the bridge, in a manner of speaking . . . it's how it *ends* that matters. I'm troubled by the same thought, he says, because the Superintendent is bound to dispatch an ambulance to fetch you back. It's his job. And she imagines a toy-sized van, a long way off, crossing a vast bare plateau. Spasms of fear and fever shake her. Well, she has a plan because she remembers Martin saying that to die of old age is the definitive mark of success. And she seems to qualify. Time to say goodbye to the epileptic girls. They cluster around her, wide-eyed and silent, their helmets soundlessly jostling and butting. But Julie stands apart and watches. Then Nurse Felicity arrives in the doorway to the Calm Down room and explains, I know you and your name means happiness.

'Does it?' Mrs Shoddy whispers.

love without hope

She burrows among bedclothes and surveys a stilled torrent of memories. She must let go of everything item by item: unforgotten hurts and surprises, fine vistas and a waterfall like fractured glass, pastures and heaped-up clouds, mental arithmetic and the stone-honed blades of a pair of scissors, a saucepan of burnt porridge, the subdivision of her land by fences and seeing her queen of spades trumped. The past is laden with pain: her father's blustering and lies, her mother's double games. The bushfire. She's glad to be rid of it. She has no system. As things pop up she gives them the flick. Even happy things, such as memories of walking round the backyard nursing a shut-eyed doll, coming upon a perfumed garden where she named the flowers, learning to knit plain and purl, steering the tractor at ten, fishing with yabbies, loving a pet mouse called Fancy – oh, all sorts of bits and bobs – tasting guava, firing her father's rifle, growing up strong, the first leg-to-leg feel of male skin, the family tradition of scanning the sky to assess the potential for rain, and breeding independent-minded horses. But she cannot bear to let go of the horses. No. Instead she burrows deeper.

And must she be without Martin, too? Of course. Martin, above all. She must cast him off like the rest, especially his endearing good humour. Yet, just thinking of him, she feels better. And reviews his lack of farming skills and how she used to mock him: I don't care how strong you are, you haven't got a clue about the way things should be done. She kisses him goodbye. Anyway, he might have died years ago for all she knows. Muffled by blankets she misses him no less keenly. But no exceptions can be allowed if she herself is to die. Last of all she calls her horses and they come tramping through the house, hoofs clamorous as jackhammers, reminding her of the days when she rode – and she could ride before she could walk – the surge of power between her thighs, that thrill of the rider elevated so far above the passing ground, the pistoning undulations of the great animal cantering across the paddocks, a breeze through her hair as she balances, rising in the stirrups, her capable sunburnt hands grasping the reins, a momentary click of the bit against the horse's teeth. Glorious. All gone now. She is empty. All but the memories from the days before memory. Waiting to be born she heard the sounds of the future through bags of mother-flesh. She lets them go now: her mother singing despite the shock of some nearby thing being smashed, the infuriated bellow of a male of the species causing Lorna's pod of succour to contract painfully, the calm rhythm of egg-beating, the turning mincer, the turning butter churn, the turning pump handle, the snickering descant of a sewing-machine needle, even though these sounds awaited explanation or *manifestation*, as Martin might say, and the predominant ever-changing and overlapping pattern woven by two hearts – hers and her mother's – pulsing in celebration of the severance to come when the first cold shock of exposure punched out the cavities of her body and a ferocious blade of daylight probed her newborn eyes.

love without hope

'Mrs Shoddy,' Gail's voice breaks in. 'Wake up, for God's sake! I had to chase Olga away. And now . . . !'

Mrs Shoddy emerges into the world as she feels her bedclothes being stripped off and she focuses with difficulty. Gail's forearm comes to rest on her lap, as heavy as the sun, a forearm sprinkled with fine golden hairs. She knows Gail, though not well. And encounters dread in the poor girl's eyes.

'Do I hear thunder?' Mrs Shoddy says.

'This is all Russell's doing,' Gail sobs.

The strange approaching roar persists.

'Nonsense, Gail,' she says, 'you're safe in my house.'

But Gail seems possessed, suddenly seizing her by the shoulders to give her a good shake and then leaping off the bed.

'You have to get up!'

'I'm trying to die.'

Somewhere Mrs Shoddy hears a door slam so violently her whole house lurches.

'You stubborn old thing,' Gail yells in terror, 'give me your arm!'

'I'm not going anywhere,' Mrs Shoddy objects, indignant and frightened.

'Come *on!*' Gail shrieks and tugs at her.

'You're too rough!'

'I'm saving you!'

Just like Vernon.

'They all say that,' Mrs Shoddy says.

So Gail lets go and blunders out by herself, out

through the scrubbed and disinfected kitchen with its reorganised store cupboard and the plentiful stocks of food she has provided for their time in hiding. She leaves the old woman waggling fragile fingers in the air and muttering objections from the squalor of her bedroom.

Coming to herself at last, Mrs Shoddy calls through the open door, 'Gail?' Then she calls out through the open window, 'Gail?'

And she struggles to prop herself on one elbow.

Martin Shoddy's heart leaps as his ute turns in at the gate, bouncing on squeaky springs, the steering wheel bucking under his hands. The all-day, all-night drive has not tired him. He doesn't tire easily. And he has knocked about all his life. Anyhow there's been plenty to think about. Archie Parker's letter, neatly folded, pokes out from his shirt pocket.

The roof of Lorna's house swings into view and the old carriage shed on the right. He kicks his vehicle up the rise, like he always did when he belonged, to watch the panorama tilt into view below him: a sudden flash-flood of green. And there it is, even more breathtaking than he remembered. But spoiled by a huge low-loader parked across the track. He slams on the brakes. Just in time to see a bulldozer crash in slow-motion against the house.

'Jesus Christ!'

The whole front wall caves and collapses as the bulldozer backs off. A moment later the roof twists askew. He throws open the car door and bounds out, lithe for his age.

'Hoy!' he bellows.

The driver in his high cabin opens a window flap. 'Keep clear,' he shouts down as he watches the intruder walk right up and place a hand on his machine.

'What the fuck are you doing?' Martin Shoddy demands.

The driver yanks his ear-muffs off. 'Come again?'

'There's been some colossal cock-up!'

The driver appraises the intruder and then appraises his ute. 'Clear out,' he snarls. 'I've got my orders.'

'So whose orders would that be?'

'Estate agent. Property's been repossessed.'

'Repossessed, my arse!' Martin Shoddy roars. 'My wife would never. Never let this place go. Never.'

By way of dismissal the driver drops the flap and revs his great motor. The bulldozer lurches and swings back to the task. The blade nudges a corner chimney – her chimney – thrusting at it till the brickwork tilts and breaks and tumbles into rubble. Martin Shoddy jumps clear – just as a door at the side of the house jerks open

love without hope

and a young woman rushes out, escaping. Hampered by her skirt, hair flying and big arms flung wide, disoriented and dazzled by sunshine, she stumbles and blunders his way.

'She...!' she shrieks right in his face, colliding with him. 'She...!'

He takes hold of her to steady her. Behind him the bulldozer revs again.

She gasps and boggles and tugs his arm.

'She's...' she shrieks again, '*in* there!'

With a massive exhalation of dust the remainder of the building lurches and begins to crumple in on itself. But Martin Shoddy already sees a tiny grey head, just visible over the sill of the open bedroom window. In a flash he is there and finds himself face to face with an unknown old woman propped up in bed. Even as his hands reach out she simply stares at him. Her eyes in their hollow sockets burn. The building groans and tilts around her.

'Can you move?' he asks.

And promptly vaults right in, barking his shins on the window frame, tripping and tumbling across the floor. He picks himself up just as the roar of the bulldozer cuts out.

'Thank Christ!' he says.

Silence.

'Martin?' the old woman asks in a normal voice.

He hobbles over and steadies himself, grasping the knob on the bed end. The hush settles. Choking with grief he bends over her.

'Is it you?' he croaks.

He plants a kiss on her forehead. And Mrs Shoddy reaches up. She clasps him. To be certain.

'I said you'd save me,' she cries.

The wreckage of the house groans.

'So, what the hell's going on?' he says.

But now she struggles against him, needing to hold him at arm's length to examine his face for some sign of the young man she lost.

'Your hair's short,' she says.

He smiles and in that moment she sees past the change in him. And he, in turn, recognises *her*.

'There's not much of you left to save,' he admits.

'Enough,' she tells him.

And, satisfied, lets him lift her off the bed.

'The poetry, though,' he says sternly, fumbling to disentangle the bedclothes from her legs, 'will have to wait.'

'I want the poetry,' she whispers like a child.

Even as they reach the bedroom door the corridor fills with bouncing chunks of mortar and a cloud of suspended brick dust.

'The whole thing's going!'

'Lord, how grey you've grown,' she remarks.

The way is blocked. Old walls and sturdy beams rise into the powdered orange light. The ceiling above them buckles and – loud as gunshots – timbers splinter to white bone. Lorna Shoddy feels herself invulnerable, with her ear against his chest, hearing his strong heartbeat just as it used to be. He turns to find another way out.

love without hope

'Martin,' she whispers.

'I know, old girl,' he confesses. 'It's been twenty years.'

With one arm he hugs her close to protect her from flying debris while with the other he pushes the window up as far as possible. She suddenly throws her head back, unbalancing them both.

'Twenty-three,' she corrects him tenderly.

The old house opens like a flower to the sun, a patch of blue widens above their heads as sheets of roof iron lift and sail slantingly aside.

'Hold tight!' he says when the whole wall shudders.

A catastrophe of sunshine avalanches around them.

'Watch out, Martin,' she warns him in a clear steady voice. 'Something's going to fall.'

NOTES & ACKNOWLEDGEMENTS

The lines quoted by Martin on page 26 are by John Manifold and reprinted by permission of the University of Queensland Press. The text on pages 133–134 is a combination of the hymn *O God our help in ages past* and words from Psalm 90. Mrs Shoddy is mistaken about the phrase she hears a bass voice singing on the car radio (page 182), it is not Russian but Polish: Penderecki's *Entombment of Christ*. Mrs Shoddy's favourite poem, which Martin begins reciting on page 190, is by Robert Graves and quoted here by permission of Penguin Books. Even in crisis, on page 268, Mrs Shoddy knows that Martin will not miss her reference to Byron's *Beppo*.

I am grateful to Victoria University for an appointment which allowed me to pay the rent while I worked on the latter stages of this book. I am grateful to my daughters, Imogen, Delia and Cressida, severally, for their ideas and the conversations which so enrich my life. To my wife, Bet, for long discussions about the idea, including the information that the Department of Lunacy was still operating into the 1980s (as was the title Master in Lunacy). To David Isaacs for his help in relation to diagnostic medicine. To the museum of Kenmore Psychiatric Hospital for many details concerning care and treatment, plus the opportunity to visit a typical ward of the period preserved as part of the museum.

My thanks to the Bundanon Trust for a four-week residency, during which most of the first draft was written, to Julian Burnside and Kate Durham for their extraordinary generosity and the use of their holiday house, where the first draft was completed. To Nadine Amadio for her enthusiasm at a time when it was much needed. To John O'Donnell, whose recording of JS Bach's *Passacaglia* (BWV 582) was playing over and over while I wrote the rain passage of Mrs Shoddy's escape from the asylum. To my friends Martin Duwell, John Stinson and Ruth Wilkinson, and to the wonderful Barbara Blackman, also to my sister, Diana Lawrence, and her husband, Barry, for their support. My thanks to Ian Dixon, who responded so warmly to the work as I first began getting it on paper, to Jarrod Boyle for back-up at various stages of the book's development, to Jo Jarrah for her productive editorial input – and to Dylan Carl, who made a huge contribution to the work in progress, sharing the energy at the Studio and working alongside me while he wrote his remarkable novel, *The Beast*.